Praise For

I0626354

THOSE POOR, POOR bastards

"This 'Dead West' series showcases just what can happen when three genius minds work together. It's unique, fresh and invigorating. *Those Poor, Poor Bastards* is full of action and unique characters intermixed with a unique spin on zombie mythology. What makes this novel even better? It's set in America's Wild West. It will sink its teeth into you and leave you wanting more. It's a crime not to read this right away."

—Sarah Chorn, Bookworm Blues

"This first book is better than *just* another Weird Western or *just* another zombie book. The writing is very visceral, raw in a style similar to Chuck Wendig...this is a high octane story [but] what makes it truly stand out among the rest is the drama between the human characters."

—Ryan Lawler, Fantasy Book Review

"*Those Poor, Poor Bastards* (the authors, as well as the book) prove that zombies and the West were made for each other, and that the undead fiends still have plenty of guts and action to offer."

—Lincoln Crisler, author of *Wild*

"Two parts bullets, three parts shambling undead, one part magic. All fast-paced Wild West action. *Dead West: Those Poor, Poor Bastards* takes you on a wild ride."

—Becca Butcher, *Voluted Tales Magazine*

THOSE POOR, POOR BASTARDS

DEAD WEST BOOK ONE

WRITTEN BY

Tim Marquitz,
J.M. Martin &
Kenny Soward

RAGNAROK PUBLICATIONS

CRESTVIEW HILLS, KENTUCKY

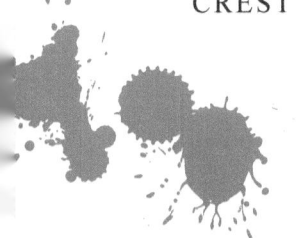

THOSE POOR, POOR BASTARDS (Dead West #1)
Ragnarok Publications | www.ragnarokpub.com
Editor In Chief: Tim Marquitz | Creative Director: J.M. Martin
Those Poor, Poor Bastards (Dead West #1) 2nd edition is copyright © 2014
by Tim Marquitz, J.M. Martin, and Kenny Soward. All rights reserved.

Published by Ragnarok Publications
206 College Park Drive, Ste. 1
Crestview Hills, KY 41017

ISBN-10: 0-9913605-2-4
ISBN-13: 978-0-9913605-2-9
Worldwide Rights
Created in the United States of America

Book design: J.M Martin
Photography: AFREEMAN Photography
Cover model: Meagan Shea Dameron

ACKNOWLEDGEMENTS

THE WRITERS WOULD LIKE TO THANK Sarah Fernandes and the Bloody Cake News, Lincoln Crisler, Tyson Mauermann, Paul Martin, Sarah Chorn, Ryan Lawler, Michael Wheeler, Melanie R. Meadors, Johnny Seabolt, Becca Butcher, and Keith West. Thank you all for spreading the love and gathering more and more readers to the Dead West cause. It is clearly our labor of love, and so are y'all.

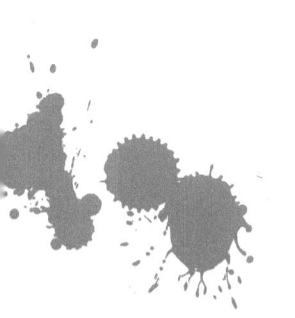

"If one of them colossal swarms come you'd hear that low rumbling noise…then jump for your horse, get to them before they scattered to hell and gone. Then you ride at a dead run in the dark if you got to, with cut banks and prairie dog holes all around. Ending up with your neck broke in a shallow grave is a damn sight better than what they'll do."

— "Teddy Blue" Abbott, *We Rode Dead West & Away From Hell*

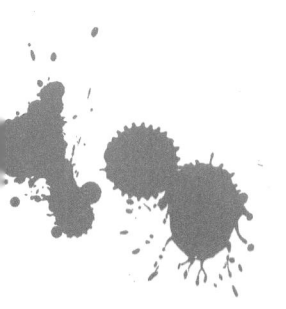

CHAPTER ONE

NINA WEAVER TUCKED AN errant strand of hair beneath her hat as the wagon trundled toward Coburn Station. It had been a long, quiet winter of deep snow and hibernating, which suited her pa just fine but sent Nina just about out of her dang skull. As much as she mistrusted so-called civilization, she'd been looking forward to doing something other than scavenging abandoned sites and dickering for fixins with brown-toothed backwoodsmen.

The wagon thumped through waterlogged ruts, jarring Nina's teeth. Pa growled and tugged the reins. All the traffic in and out of the little road ranch-turned-trade town, along with the thaw, had churned the rail-side road to damn sposh.

Speaking of the rail, Nina had kept one eye on it, hoping to catch sight of one of them iron horseys of the Central

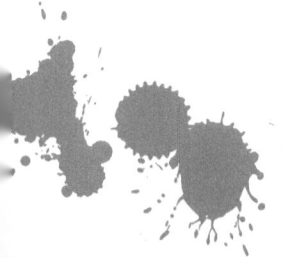

Pacific line up close. She marveled at the thing, and felt a little pride in her white blood; the occasional cosmopolitan flash of *wasichu* inventiveness and her pa's poetic heart but hard-as-iron exterior was pretty much the extent of her pride.

Nina's gaze swept over the town. Past the buildings, on the hillside above and to her right, the labor camp seemed in a ruckus. A few dozen coolies were rushing about—she knew they were Celestials 'cause of their blue-dyed pajama clothes and bamboo hats.

"What you reckon the hellabaloo is over yonder?" Nina said. They both sat up front, side by side.

"What's that?" Pa was busy chirking and tugging at Apple's and Oatmeal's reins. He looked over.

"Thataway." Nina jerked her chin toward the tents on the hill and all the Chinamen scurrying about.

Pa squinted and shook his head, returned his attention to the road as they passed by the first timber frame building, a pair of colored laborers and one white fella were banging away at it and paused to look them over.

Nina turned her head down, avoiding their stares.

"Maybe there's a work order or an assembly or something," Pa said. "Hard tellin."

They rode on into town and Pa pulled the wagon between a couple clapboard buildings, told her to keep an eye on things and out of trouble. He grabbed two canvas bags and tossed them over his shoulder. "I'll be back in less than an hour. Just you lay low, all right?"

Nina nodded.

"Got the piece I gave you?"

"Yup."

He nodded and squeezed her shoulder. "Business as usual, Nina girl."

"Hurry back," she said, a little disappointed he didn't take her with him.

After ten minutes of leaning against the wagon, Nina decided stepping out onto the street to catch a glimpse of things wouldn't hurt. She'd been shut in all winter, after all, and it sounded like Pa didn't intend to stick around overlong.

Her boots squelched in the mud and the stench of horse shit burned her nostrils. This part of Main Street was even worse than the outskirts; a god-awful mess of manure and mud, a damned bonafide wagon trap, like some thick river of organic slop only a pig could love.

A pair of stinky traders passed by on the wooden-planked walkway, each with a string of carcasses slung over their shoulders. They nodded at Nina. She nodded back, keeping her brim low. On a bench next door, a couple old-timers cackled and spat baccy far as they could into the street. Across the filth-ridden lane, two girls of the line hawked themselves in front of the Pussy Palace, flirting with their lips and stockinged legs, lifting their dingy dresses sky high. Another whore tossed a bucket of piss from the second story window while one of her *sisters* priced cunt to a man on the boardwalk just below. He hopped back and cursed the piss-thrower.

More laborers banged wooden frames together at the far end of Main Street, real structures to replace the tent city that had originally accommodated the growing town. Dogs barked, pots and pans rattled against the sides of wagons, and men shouted at one another as if they were in a competition to see who could wake the fucking dead.

She remembered now why she hated towns. Civilization was too goddamned noisy. Nina shook her head and leaned against the corner of the building. She pulled a quirley from the top pocket of her overalls, lit it, took a puff, stifled a cough. Too much damn smoke. She covered her mouth to hide her discomfort.

Not only did she hate towns, she hated cigarettes, too.

Business as usual, Nina girl. Her job was to watch the goods while Pa, always the crafty salesman, worked his magic on the proprietor of Smith & Towne's Antiquities. If things worked out, they'd take their earnings to the general store and get a fair shake on some supplies. They needed salted pork, bread and cheese, a fruit or two, and a new ax; if they had enough left, maybe they'd procure a few sketchy items, as well, from the back alleys and shacks around town. Those would take a special kind of dickering, meetings under the cover of darkness, and a shit-ton of balls.

Another part of Nina's job was to not look like Nina. That is, a half-Injun with long legs and a full pair of tits. Bad blood was everywhere; war between this tribe and that, and the danged Army was posting pony at fifty *dineros* a head, no matter the tribe. Natives were striking back hard these days too, raiding U.S. patrols along the Snake River for a couple seasons now. She and Pa wanted no part of that. They'd not seen her mother's people in years, not since Ma's spirit had passed on from this world; so, long story short, if anyone recognized Nina as anything other than imported help, she was ought to be raped or scalped or both.

She took comfort in the Colt 1861 Navy beneath her

coat, the piece Pa had mentioned. It was his iron, from back in his scouting days, but he usually let her carry it, and she'd not hesitate if anyone started up trouble. Speaking of which, she spied a man eyeballing her from across the street as folks hustled past. His feet crossed in front of him, he leaned against a pole in front of the Nugget Saloon, as casual as could be, holding a quirley by his waist between draws, and making no attempt to hide his curiosity. He wore his hat tilted forward, shading his eyes, but Nina could make out the shadow of stubble framing his jaw and a thick, dark mustache over his upper lip.

"Where you from, stranger?" Another man surprised her, having walked up and stopped two paces away. A big-eared, screw-mouthed fella. He flicked ashes into the mud and put his cigar between his teeth. "I've been in Truckee forty-some days. Ain't never seen you around."

Nina knew the accent. South. *Deep South.* She'd been to Alabama once. It was the kind of drawl that made her think of cotton fields and black, sweaty faces. So, it didn't surprise her that this man, after noticing her copper complexion, had come to see what he could fuck with. Or maybe he was just being neighborly. Never could tell.

Nina spoke in her rehearsed tone, the deepest baritone she could muster without sounding like a put-on. "Truckee? I thought they called this place Coburn Station."

"Used to. Not no more. So you're new here?"

"Just rolled in. Gettin' supplies."

"Ah. What kind of...*supplies* you lookin' for? Might have some things can't be found at the general. And especially not at this fuckin' Jew cunt's place." He motioned at the antiquities shop behind them.

Nina's stomach flipped. A trap. If she pursued his offer, he could turn her in to the law. Maybe he *was* the law, although he didn't look the part, with his threadbare jacket and cotton trousers. She couldn't see evidence of a gun on him, but that didn't mean he was unarmed. If she told him to skedaddle, he'd have even more reason to be curious about her.

"Been coming here for years. Off and on." She chanced a glance at him, just as he glanced at her. His eyes were that dangerous combination of ignorance and predatory hate. He was the sort of mean man Nina and her pa had experienced many times in their travels.

She might be in a bit of trouble with this one.

Nina hoped he couldn't see past her dirt-rubbed cheeks and tar-blackened teeth, the disguise she wore whenever entering wasichu's world, but her confidence was shot to pieces when the man pulled his cigar, gave a greasy smile, and rolled his tongue out over his lips.

Definitely trouble.

She took a draw from her cigarette and glanced across the street at Mustache. He hadn't moved. Maybe this *wasn't* a two-man operation. Maybe Mustache just wanted to watch the show.

Meany's eyes narrowed. He edged closer. "So you, uh… it's just you and your pa?"

Nina took a step back toward the wagon, blowing out a slow cloud of smoke as if she could hide behind it. "Yup."

"Well, ain't that somethin'?" He glanced around furtively, backing her up. It was only a matter of time before he made his move. "See, I'm what you might call a perceptive fella. Up here in the mountains, you got to know about rocks, see? Whether you're mining or blastin' a hole in them, or just havin' a look at what's underneath. Most rocks, they always got somethin' underneath, see?"

"Why don't you do your prospecting somewhere else?"

He stuck his cigar between his teeth, took another step forward, got uncomfortably close. Nina's palms itched for the handle of the pistol in her coat. "You just got to lift them rocks up and have a look," Meany said. "That's why I come over here. I lifted…" He reached out and tipped the brim of her hat up. "And look what I found, a pretty little Injun girl…"

A commotion at the far end of town interrupted him; a chorus of dogs barking, howling, and yipping all at once. An unnatural shiver ran down Nina's spine, and the danger Meany posed felt lessened in comparison, which was mighty peculiar.

She walked around him to have a look, checking him with her shoulder as she went by. He was skin and bones beneath his coat, but he did indeed have a pistol ferreted away in a shoulder holster. He grunted and stepped back— only one thing a violent fellow like this understood, and that was greater violence. Nina would have to dish him some if need be, but that wasn't her primary concern right now.

What was happening at the far end of Main?

She rounded the corner of the building and jerked back as a pack of dogs ran by, mongrels with matted coats and patches of mange, yelping like they were being beaten to within an inch of their lives. She chanced a second look as two more packs scurried past.

The wagon shimmied and shook as her horses, Apple and Oatmeal, pulled nervously in their tugs. Nina turned and ran smack into Meany. She didn't know if this was his move, or if he was just curious about the noise, too, but she wasn't waiting to find out. She hooked a foot behind his legs, grabbed the front of his shirt, and shoved him into the mud.

Without waiting to see his reaction, Nina hopped the boardwalk and went to the front of the wagon. She took hold of Apple's reins to calm the old boy, even as he continued to nicker and paw the ground.

"C'mon," she urged, guiding the horses halfway out from between the buildings. She wanted to be ready to skedaddle as soon as Pa returned. This ruckus, along with her encounter with Meany, had made her mind up; she'd had enough of Coburn Station.

More commotion was happening at the far end of Main Street. An old covered wagon resting across the lane took a battering from some unseen force. It vibrated and bumped around, suddenly flying up, flipping on its side, and falling to pieces.

Horses and cows poured over and around the crushed parts and stampeded down the street, flying with reckless abandon, churning up mud as they came, crazed eyes spinning around in their tossing heads. Nina's first thought was that they were infected with something. What did they call it? Rabies?

One man ran to the middle of the lane and held up his hands as if to stop the oncoming horde.

Don't do that, mister.

A young bull lowered his head and barreled over the man, sending him careening down the lane where he landed hard on his back. Blood covered his face and lips, but he was still alive. He looked up just as the herd ran him over, crushing him to pieces beneath tons of panicked flesh.

Nina glanced across the way, catching Mustache's eye just as the herd raced by. She probably mirrored his expression, neither of them ever having seen so many spooked animals. She blinked, and Mustache was gone.

Time to haul ass. They could come back some other time when things were less out of hand. She turned and found her path blocked again by Meany. "Now look here, yo—," he started, but Nina punched him in the nose. He staggered back two paces and clutched his face, eyes watering.

"Hey!" he cried, a muffled sound. She saw his hand move toward his coat.

She pulled her Colt and squared at his chest, cocked the weapon and gave him a final warning, no longer concerned with disguising her voice. "I'll put a bullet in the same spot if you don't back the fuck off, mister. You think I'm joking just..."

Nina stopped, her threat falling short. The man's eyes were opened wide, his mouth an O behind his hand. He wasn't looking at Nina or her gun. He wore an expression of dumb terror; something was scaring the hell out of the sumbitch. Something *behind* her. Going against one of her golden rules—once you pull you never take your gun off the enemy till they're either dead or gone from sight—she turned and gave pause.

Rambling down the street after the panicked herd was another pack of animals. Injured horses bled from horrendous cuts, gashes, and tears. Horseflesh hung in swaths, muzzles chewed to the bone as if crows had been at them for a week. One beast was half-skinned, the fibrous muscles of its shoulder and hind quarters painfully visible, glistening with congealed blood. A second animal had a rip down its side, eviscerated, dragging its bowels through the mud. Another disturbing thing—just a small bit of non-horse fucking behavior that stuck in Nina's craw— they had no breath; no billowing, nostril-flaring puffs of steam an equine with heaving sides might display in the cold, spring air.

The herd cantered along on unsteady legs, bumping against one another as pieces of loose skin and gristle sloughed off into the mud. A lumbering, silent mass of dead meat.

Nina backed away from the unholy sight, suddenly wishing she'd listened to her mother's religious convictions, for surely she must have died and taken an express train straight to Hell.

CHAPTER TWO

NINA STRUGGLED TO MAKE sense of what she saw when Oatmeal kicked and whinnied, rearing up, twisting and busting the tug from his collar with a *snap*. The wooden trace struck Nina in the shoulder, knocking her on her ass.

"Nina!" Pa came rushing up. "What in the blazes—"

A tremendous, half-ton draft horse made a direct line for the wagon. Its tongue lolled from the rotting hole in its cheek. One pus-filled eye bulged from its socket. Stained yellow teeth gnashed together with an unsettling *clacking* sound, and the sweet stench of decay ran before it like a foul wind.

Nina felt strong hands slip under her arms and lift her up. Not fast enough.

The putrefied horse smashed into Oatmeal with the heavy thud of meat against meat. Oatmeal's legs slid to the side, tangling him in his leather harness and pinning him beneath the draft horse's weight. The raging beast made a disturbing nickering sound and clamped its teeth to the nape of Oatmeal's neck, tore out a chunk of flesh, stretching skin and gristle in a spray of blood. Oatmeal screamed, legs flailing and kicking, showering Nina and Pa with rancid muck. Nina wiped her hand across her face, succeeding only in spreading the stink of dirt and manure across her cheeks.

"Shoot it before it kills Oatmeal!" Pa shouted as the beast tore another bite out of their horse.

Nina raised her gun and put a bullet in the beast's neck. The round had no effect, leaving only a blood-leaking pinhole. It was like shooting a damn tree. Nina sighted for another shot, but Apple reared and flailed with his hooves, slicing the beast's rotted muzzle to the bone; one of its ears tore free and spun away.

Apple hit the ground and bucked sideways against his trace. Nina put the next round in the wicked thing's head, exploding bone fragments and brains everywhere. It staggered and went down, landing with a *thwump* in the mud.

Nina took stock of the situation. Screams and gunshots rang out. People scattered as crazed animals rampaged through town. Across the lane, a woman in petticoats ran down the boardwalk, pursued by a clumsy, three-legged stallion nipping at her skirts. At the end of the track she slipped and tumbled, hitting the mud face-first. The beast landed atop her, stomping, peeling off strips of skin with its sharp incisors as the woman screamed.

"Nina, help me settle 'em down and get Oatmeal re-hitched," Pa said, reaching down to check the injured horse.

She nodded, looking around for Meany. Nowhere to be found.

Nina hurried to the back of the wagon to see the street. "We need to get turned around. It's the only way outta here," she said. Otherwise, they'd have to grab some necessaries and manage on foot. Whatever was going on, they couldn't stay in this hellish place.

A man ran from an alley, chased by a pack of gnashing dogs on stiff, jerky legs. Their howls wormed into Nina's ears and set her hands to shaking. The man made it to the middle of the street before the dogs pulled him down. They bit into him, dragging apart his arms and legs, tearing into his belly, plunging their muzzles deep inside to feast. His screams withered amid a chorus of gurgles and growls. Crimson foam welled from his mouth.

Nina just couldn't quite reckon it. She'd raised her gun, then lowered it. Poor bastard was already dead. Hardly thinking, she reached into the back of the wagon and pulled out a pouch of rounds, hooking the strap over her shoulder.

"Nina!"

Pa clung to Oatmeal's bridle, half-dragged into the street, feet buried in the muck, trying to keep the injured horse calm. Only problem was Apple shared Oatmeal's sentiment, and both wanted to get the fuck out of Coburn. Nina couldn't blame them, but she'd never get Pa into the moving wagon.

"It's okay, Oatmeal," she cooed, putting her arm around the horse's neck, one hand clutching his bridle as they were pulled along. "Settle down, boy. Let's get you situated, and then I prom—"

Pa grunted, a hard man for his fifty-odd years of frontier living, but not strong enough to hold a wagon horse. Oatmeal's coat was slick with blood, which made it all the harder. One of Pa's hands draped across the horse's neck, the other across the top of his snout, as he did his damndest to cover Oatmeal's eyes.

For a brief moment, Nina thought they might win. Oatmeal stopped tugging, and the wagon settled to a stop. She was about to tell Pa to get in, when a shotgun went off nearby. Oatmeal jerked from Nina's grasp and strained against the wagon's weight. Apple kicked, and together the horses sped off. Pa went face-first into the muck. Nina slipped, too, her hand grasping the raw wound on Oatmeal's neck for a split second before losing her grip and landing on her backside. They watched as their supplies trundled down the lane through the chaos and disappeared around the bend.

"*Goldernit,*" Pa sputtered, wiped his mouth on his coat sleeve.

Nina rolled over and snatched the dropped Colt from the mud, wiped it on her sleeve, and went to help her father. "You got your gun, Pa?"

"I got it. Sorry, Nina. I couldn't…" He shook his head and grit his teeth.

"Not your fault, Pa, but we gotta get off this street. All Hell's done broke loose."

"Looks that way. Let's get back inside Smith's."

Nina led the way up on to the walk, turned the brass knob of Smith & Towne's Fineries and pushed the door.

It didn't budge. She threw her shoulder against the rough wood and met solid resistance. She stepped back. A closed sign swayed in the front window.

Pa slapped his hand on the siding and yelled, "John Smith, open up! I just cut you a hell of a deal on that cutlery set."

Nina heard scratching, claws against wood, then something huge slammed into her from the side. She tumbled, landing on her shoulder, and smacking her chin. She brought up her gun just as two paws struck her chest, followed by a slavering maw, long canines descending like the teeth of a dern bear trap. Nina grabbed a handful of shaggy hair and slammed the butt of her pistol against the dog's head once, twice, three times, all to no effect. The thing's fetid breath rolled over her, made her gag. Nina fired her weapon point blank, unsure if she hit anything. The teeth snapped again, nearly clipping her nose. She realized Pa was kicking the shit out of it, screaming her name.

Suddenly, the weight was gone. Nina sucked in a deep breath and saw a man holding the dog by its scruff and rump. He heaved the big hound off the walk and into the mud, pulled a pistol, and shot it through the eye before it had stopped sliding. They all watched a moment to make sure the dog was dead. The man holstered his weapon, turned and clapped Pa on the shoulder.

Pa nodded and took a breath while the stranger offered his hand to Nina. She hesitated before she accepted. The man brought her quick to her feet with a solid pull.

It was Mustache. He tipped his hat and gave Nina a crooked smile. Handsome, though. She stopped herself thinking that and muttered her thanks.

"C'mon." Mustache walked east, away from the general store and the finery shop, striding with calm, reserved confidence. He stuck close to the buildings and checked around corners before moving ahead. It looked like he'd done some sneaking a time or two in his life, so Nina was fine following a few steps behind. She wasn't sure if they could trust him, but alternatives seemed few and far between.

A dense fog rolled down Main from the direction the horses had vanished, seeping between buildings and feeling its way around like a blind, hungry beast. Even the sky darkened; a black blanket of clouds rolling in above them, as if God had passed judgment on Coburn Station and sentenced the pisswater hole to death by suffocation.

Nina noticed the sounds of terror had faded, leaving behind an eerie quiet. Their footsteps on the boardwalk resounded. Pa had his five-shot Cooper pointed skyward, and she knew he had another stowed in his hip pocket holster.

Two dogs slunk along the street, stalking, growling with red-stained muzzles. Pa drew on them, but Mustache whipped out a second six-shooter and blew the hounds away with two quick shots. Mustache spit through a haze of gun smoke.

"Ain't seen too many can sling that fast," said Pa.

Nina narrowed her eyes at the man, then considered the dead dogs.

"Name's Manning. James Manning."

"Lincoln Weaver. This here's my daughter, Nina."

"Lincoln. Nina. Pleasure. Now let's begone."

They continued down the boardwalk, passing the boot

store and slaughter barn. Smells of carcasses teetering on the edge of decay plucked at their noses. The flat, coppery scent of blood. Slavering grunts met their ears. They passed quietly, attracting no attention from the things feasting on fresh-slaughtered animals.

They hunkered down in front of the door to the law office. Nina shoved, but it was locked; probably barred, too. They *could* break in, creating some noise, maybe get shot in the process.

Manning whispered to no one in particular. "What on God's earth is going on?"

"Hell if I know," said Nina. "You got any kind of plan, Mister Manning?"

He fixed her with a look. She took note of his dark hair, sweaty beneath his hat, eyes the color of blue stone, then made herself stop. *Again.*

Th'hell's wrong with me, and with all this going on…

"Alright, Nina, Mister Weaver—"

"Just Lincoln."

"Fair enough, Lincoln. I figure we cross over to the other side and see if anyone's guarding the stables. If there's a horse left alive, we're gonna need—"

Ragged screams grabbed their attention. From the fog came Oatmeal and Apple, pulling the wagon behind them, the canvas cover blazing like a reckless comet. The horses careened to their side of the street, the wagon clacking and creaking.

"Someone must have shot it up," Pa said, shaking his head and looking for something to duck behind. Nina pursed her lips, tugging Manning's coat sleeve and pulling him behind a couple water barrels, silently shooing their poor horses away. "Get down," she hissed.

Manning looked all quizzical.

"There's powder on that wagon."

"Oh." He ducked.

Thankfully, Apple and Oatmeal rushed by without the wagon erupting. They peeked over the barrels as the horses struggled and bucked back across the street, a pounding, out-of-control mass of wood and horseflesh weaving in front of the Pony Express post. The horses banked right, hit a rut, and Nina gasped as the wagon keeled on two wheels for several yards, then it overbalanced and exploded against the wooden poles holding up the livery office porch.

A ball of fire plumed. The concussion rocked the ground. Nina felt the heat all the way to their hiding spot. Debris whizzed by, landing in the mud with *thunks*. The smells of charred wood, powder, and cooked horse burned her eyes. The livery office blazed; the stable roof was on fire, too.

"There goes that idea." Pa stood and frowned at the conflagration. "All Coburn will go up in flames in minutes. If there were any horses alive in there…"

"Ain't all we got to worry about, Lincoln."

They followed Manning's nod, looked down the street where a dark shadow came pressing down from the west. Beneath its oppressiveness, folks ambled in the capering fog, forty or fifty strong; men and women, gunshot or hacked, afflicted with grievous wounds that should have killed them; yet, they stood, bleeding and warped, teeth gnashing like those sick dogs and horses, a small army of persistent flesh. Some looked recently dug up, skin glowing gray in the mist, hair hanging in patches from skull-bare heads.

Nina felt sick. Her gut screamed at her to flee. "Pa.

Mister Manning..."

"I'm there with ya, darlin'," Manning said.

The three of them backed away, boots creaking on the wooden boards. Several pairs of rheumy eyes among the legion of...*undead*...turned their way. Nina cupped her hands over her ears as a collective moan went up.

Pa took aim, but then drew back. "Too many. Whatever the hell they are."

Nina looked at her father. "What do we do?"

"Run," he said.

Then two cadaverous claws broke through the store window behind James Manning and took hold of his shoulders.

CHAPTER THREE

Nina hollered and kicked at the grasping arms. Her heavy boot snapped one at the elbow and pinned both limbs against the opposite side of the windowsill. Manning spun free and fired a shot through the window, sending the grabby bastard reeling.

"Appreciate it," Manning said with a nod.

Before Nina could reply, the door to the law office flew open and a fine-dressed gentleman-type barged through, locked his hands around Pa's throat. The gent had mindless eyes and gray skin just like the others, but close up, Nina saw an unholy fever, too; angry red pimples all spattered across his face and neck, oozing pustules of pale discharge.

Pa put his fists together and shoved upwards, knocking the man's hands away, and hit him in the face with the butt

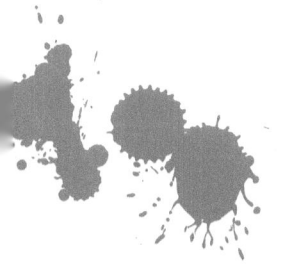

of his gun. His bulbous nose exploded like a ripe tomato. Nina put her gun to his temple and told herself it's either this lunatic or her pa; she squeezed the trigger, coating the law office's facing with the gent's blood and brains. He buckled and hit the ground like a sack of grain.

"That's…that's Eli Frankel…" Pa looked down at the dead gent. He swallowed hard.

Not anymore it ain't, Nina thought.

"He and I go back a ways." Pa sighed and shook his head a little. "Damn. What is happening to these poor people?"

"These aren't people," Nina said. Whoever they might have been once was gone now. They had become voracious, persistent *things*. Got no feelings or needs Nina could fathom, other than biting and tearing the nearest living thing to gory pieces.

Pa looked at her. "Don't say that."

"She might be right," said Manning. "They look like walking dead to me. Ain't no way your pal Frankel would have come at us if he was still breathing. I put lead right through his throat and he still came milling for us."

"C'mon then," Pa said. He led them east along the boardwalk, trying to put some distance between themselves and the shambling forms. "All I'm saying is Eli was fine just a half-hour ago. We had coffee."

"What do you think it is then, Pa?"

"Might be we're dealing with some kind of sickness," Manning said.

"I won't disagree with that," Pa said. "That seems the likeliest explanation, ask me."

Nina glanced back at the *deaduns*, moaning and glaring with their voracious hunger. She gulped. They weren't fast, but they weren't slow, neither. "What kind of sickness makes the dead walk then?"

No one could answer that perplexing question, but Pa had another. "How many people you reckon were *alive* in Coburn before all this?"

Manning answered, "I'd say two-thousand, maybe another thousand or two in the surrounds. Lots of coolies laying track way down east of Summit and such."

"And we know whatever this ruckus is…people who were otherwise healthy got it, and fast, too." Pa paused, fixing to check around a corner. "If it spreads like that…"

Nina got his point, and she was sure Manning did too.

"We don't have that many bullets, Lincoln."

A half-dozen forms emerged from the alley ahead. They surged forward, arms outstretched, fingers locked into claws in a semblance of living rigor mortis.

Pa fired twice. One fell. Manning backed into the street and dropped two more in as many shots. Glass broke and Nina heard some shuffling on the awning above. She looked up; a form stood precariously on the edge, teetering forward, hands outstretched. It took a step into space, crashing to the ground beside her. Without thinking, Nina lifted her boot and stomped his head, repeatedly, her hard soles sloughing off pieces of dark hair and flesh as the thing gargled on mud. Her last stomp slid down the skull and snapped its backbone.

Pa fired another shot. Nina looked to see a Chinaman just ten feet away, coming for her, a blood-gushing bullet hole in the side of his neck. She raised her gun, but the man's windmilling arms knocked her back, nearly tripping her over the poor bastard she'd just boot-stomped. Nina steadied herself in the slick muck, grabbed the man's arm, twisted and yanked, using his momentum to throw him to the ground. She stepped forward and blew his brains through the front of his skull, turning the mud to rust.

She looked up as Manning dropped another Chinese laborer two steps before it reached him, then saw Pa having some trouble. A monstrous woman in a filthy nightgown had a handful of his coat. Her head jutted forward, teeth chomping for his face. Pa dropped his gun and craned his head away from those clacking teeth, keeping himself stiff-legged as he could, but the woman was huge and pushed him through the mud.

"Get this behemoth off me!" Pa's face purpled with effort as he struggled against those meaty arms.

"Hold on!" Only one bullet remained in her Navy and, besides that, she didn't want to risk shooting her father instead. She switched her gun to her off-hand and pulled her hunting knife.

Where was the softest spot? Nina turned slightly left, reverse-gripped her knife and whipped it backhanded, burying the blade three-quarters deep into the woman's temple. She collapsed back to dead.

Pa rolled the large woman off. "Good girl," he said, standing up and sucking wind.

"Sorry, Pa. Just got one bullet left."

Manning handed Pa's weapon to him. "She's got a point," he said. "We need more rounds. Could stand to have an ax or two."

The main horde that had been trailing them had closed within thirty to forty feet now, lots of Celestials, and sudden panic welled up inside Nina. That might explain all the ruckus she'd seen uphill when they rolled into town. They must've been dealing with some kind of outbreak, and now they'd all spilled down into Coburn proper.

She took a deep breath and sighted up the nearest Chinaman.

Pa touched her on the arm. "Let's just get a move on. They ain't stoppin' and neither can we."

She nodded and tucked her pistol.

They proceeded slow but steady down Main, staying ahead of the shambling masses. "Stick to the middle," Pa said. "Anything might come outta those alleys and buildings. Stay sharp."

"You got a destination in mind?" asked Manning.

"East is all I got at the moment. I'm thinkin'."

The conflagration was consuming everything along the left side of the street, burning its way to the end. Nina wondered when it would spread to the other side, trapping them between twin Hells. What if they made it out of town? What then? What if the deaduns followed and hunted them down in the cold woods? Nina shivered.

"Hey! You seein' what I'm seein'?" Manning pointed at a covered supply wagon, overturned in the middle of the lane to their right, several wares all tumbled out into the street.

"Yes, sir," Pa said. "I say we help ourselves. I reckon we could make do with a quick breather too, before the fire comes thisaway."

Manning opened the front flap, lifting the splintered wood of the collapsed cover, while Pa checked the back. Nina took a moment to reload her weapon, placing five paper cartridges into the empty chambers and packing them down with the loading lever. Her hands shook as she placed her caps, so she kept one thumb on the hammer to avoid blowing her own tits off.

"Got an ax here, couple decent knives, and a rifle," Manning called out. "No loadin' pouch though...wait, here it is."

Pa made a frustrated sound. "Can't find a dern thing back here. Goldern mess of clothes done spilled out over everything. Nina girl, you wanna try on some dresses?"

Nina grunted.

"I didn't think so."

She finished loading and glanced up with a smile, which quickly evaporated when she saw two deaduns coming. "Pa!" She moved around for a better shot.

Pa's rump stuck out the back of the wagon, one leg kicking out like a mule even as one undead bent, grasping at it. Nina shot the other in the jaw, teeth and bone shattering, sending the bald bastard reeling into the mud.

The one on Pa caught his ankle with two hands, twisting it. Pa screamed and flipped on his back, kicking. The thing's legs got swept out, and it landed on him, taking up a mouthful of Pa's trousers near his crotch, shaking its head like a dog with a bone. Nina angled for a shot but reckoned Pa wouldn't appreciate a bullet near the nethers.

Pa beat at it with one fist and reached into the wagon with the other. He brought out a cast iron frying pan and clobbered the deadun in the head until he—*it?*—stopped moving.

Manning pulled it off, and Nina's stomach sank at her father's grimace.

"I think my damn foot's broke."

Manning took a quick peek and nodded but made no

other comment.

Nina peered up the street. A smoky haze covered much of the ground, dozens of deaduns drawing closer, backlit by the hungry flames. A woman with loose strands of mucus hanging from her nose led the pack. She glared from eyes the color of black quartz. This one seemed different than the others.

"I see you," the woman croaked, reaching with cracked, black fingernails.

Nina had a bead on her but hesitated. They could speak?

Manning shot the woman in the face, blowing brainy detritus into the pack behind her. Without batting an eye, he yelled, "Let's get around the other side of the wagon. Help me with your father."

Manning grabbed Pa beneath the arms and Nina behind his knees. They situated him into a standing position, leaning against the wooden flatbed. She and Manning flanked him and put their weapons on the side rail, laying out all the extra rounds they had.

"We got about twenty seconds," Manning said with a surprising amount of calm as he checked the rifle he'd pilfered from the wagon. "So get ready."

Turned out to be less than that as one of the deaduns, a dandy of a man with a button-up coat and sprung collar, tried climbing over the crushed wagon to get at them. Pa put a bullet square in his chest, knocking him back off the wagon, but the dandy came on, tripping and falling into the canvas between the wagon's ribs. Pa's gun sparked again and the man's head blossomed like a split melon, soaking the canvas red.

Nina shook her head. Deaduns were tough but none

too bright, that was for sure.

"Gotta get'em in the head," Manning shouted. "Closest ones first." He popped off a shot. Nina and Pa followed suit, picking targets and firing. Nina fed off the two men's calm deliberation, sighting one creature after another and emptying her six rounds.

Pop! A bullet blew the top off a blond girl's head.

Pop! Another round demolished a man's jaw in a cloud of bone and blood, and Nina watched his head roll off his shoulders and down his chest, leaving a trail of slime behind. A boy, no older than twelve lurched forward.

She swallowed down her moral compunctions. *It's them or us.*

The air snapped with gunfire, her vision obscured by clouds of black powder and gun smoke. She reloaded, emptied, and reloaded again. There was no sign of letting up. Droves of deaduns came from every direction, their moans swelling into a chorus of bloodthirsty need that drowned out the gunfire.

"We can't stay here," Manning finally yelled. "Lincoln, are you able to walk?" The gunfighter—for evidently that's what he was, Nina reckoned, as he was fast as lightning and never missed—fired his final rifle shot and snatched up one of his dragoons.

Pa tried some weight on his foot and flashed his teeth. "Dern it!" He looked at Nina and took a breath. "If I gotta, I gotta. Let's scoot."

Nina put down one more closing deadun, pulled her pouch over her shoulder, and got under Pa's arm. They took three steps before his weight bore them to the ground. Nina struggled to pull him up but he pushed her away. His blue-gray eyes held hers with a familiar determination, a look that told her he wouldn't be disobeyed.

"Nina, you've got to go. Both of you."

"That ain't happenin'." She shook her head. "Now come on before they're on us."

"Nina, leave me be."

She frowned and stood, shot a black man in a pair of worker's overalls coming around the wagon. The top of his skull flew up like a patch of shoveled earth, yet more of the moaning bastards crushed in behind him.

With two rounds left and no time to reload, Nina knew they'd had it. She glanced at Manning, who fired another shot and looked her in the eyes. He was half leaning—ready to bolt—but something kept him rooted. She didn't have time to ponder it.

"I'm not goin'!" Nina hollered at her pa. She bent down and lifted him by the arm. "You're all I got. Now get your ass under cover."

Nina helped Pa drag-crawl back to the wagon, and she went for the long-handled ax. Manning stood nearby, holding his rifle by the barrel. He winked and gave her a crooked smile before taking a huge swing at another big, lumbering Negro deadun coming around the side. The pointed edge of the stock smashed him in the temple and dropped him like a tipped cow. The bastard was so big, he made a decent barricade; two snarling Chinamen in their blood-spattered blue pajamas fell over him, and Manning dispatched them with brutal blows to the backs of their skulls from the rifle's butt.

A pang of regret lodged in Nina's throat as she hefted the ax. She'd spent most of her growing years hunting and gutting animals, so her hands were strong and capable, but these weren't no rabbit or fox. She gave herself plenty of room and squared off with the dozen or so coming around on her side.

"Alright, you bastards, let's go."

The first one was a bullet-riddled Chinaman, so she cut low and half severed his neck, just managing to shut her eyes as his blood sprayed her face. A reverse swing finished the job, dropping him lop-headed and lifeless against the wagon wheel. She continued like that; breathing, cutting, killing, feeling the impact of the ax head against skulls, crushing bone and brains like putrid melons. A strange sense of calm overtook her. It was easy when you knew you were done and dead. Panic fell away like dirt after a bath. She felt pure, powerful.

A young girl in gore-stained finery stepped over the five or six bodies at Nina's feet, getting in too close for comfort. Nina couldn't swing on her so she used the haft of the ax to push her away, her boots slipping in the mud and blood. She nearly went down, but recovered just in time to block the groping, snarling child-thing. The girl slipped and fell, too. Nina swore and buried her ax in the poor child's face. She swore again, angry for having to kill another kid, but she had about two damn seconds to think about it as the moaning hordes kept coming.

After she felled four or five more, her arms and hands ached. Her legs shook from trying to stay upright in the slop. Shots went off behind her. Sounded like Pa's Cooper. She was too exhausted to look back, check on Manning. The realization struck home; she couldn't run away even if she wanted to.

A tall woman with mucky auburn tresses and a black corset—probably one of the Pussy Palace whores—kicked one of the hacked up bodies aside and stumbled forward, mumbling gibberish and dripping runnels of drool from her chin.

"Ma," Nina whispered as she clumsily brought up her ax, tears in her eyes from all this ferocious and terrible madness that transcended every nightmare she'd ever had. "I'm sorry..."

The woman's head suddenly pitched sideways, a gush of gore exiting the new hole there. Her groin jerked and her semi-white bloomers flowered with blood. Nina looked around in bewilderment as the woman collapsed.

A familiar-looking man ran up. Through the grime on his face she recognized that screw-mouth and predatory eyes: the mean Southerner from just before all this shit started. He came hooting and hollering like he'd just found him a tick of Comstock silver. "Hell yeah!" Meany slammed his foot down on the dead woman's chest. "Sorry, ma'am, but you done been cunt shot! Woo!"

Another man strode up with considerably less bustle, giving off the same vigor, only his rowdiness was toned down a notch; in fact, his demeanor seemed downright cool, his mustached lips wrapped around a billowing cigar. He had a rough jaw and big ears, and there was no mistaking these two for brothers, only this one dressed cleaner; matching pants and vest and a flat-topped hat. Remarkably spotless, given the circumstances.

The brothers cocked and fired into the groaning crowd, their Spencer carbines blazing, dropping deaduns in an impressive display of marksmanship.

The second fellow relaxed his shooting pose and looked back where they'd come from. "Goddamn it, Nancy, pony up already, girl!" Then he turned and noticed Nina for the first time, narrowed his eyes. "Whoa, now. Heads up, George."

Meany, who appeared to be named George, glanced at Nina, then his face balled up before a grin widened it, and his eyes crawled her up and down. "Lookee! That's the half-breed bitch socked me one in the beezer."

Nina fixed a hard gaze on both of them and hefted her ax. "I'll do it again you fellas don't get a move on."

The brothers glanced at one another, then Mean George spat and leveled his carbine right at her.

CHAPTER FOUR

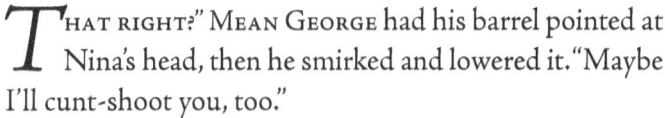

*T*HAT RIGHT?" MEAN GEORGE had his barrel pointed at Nina's head, then he smirked and lowered it. "Maybe I'll cunt-shoot you, too."

"You best back off, son." Pa trained his pistol on the man. Nina didn't know how many shots he had left, but they wouldn't stand a chance against those Spencers.

Mean George scooted closer, eyes spitting fire. "I'll square you both away right now. Put a bullet in your pa's head, and you..." He licked his lips and pumped his hips. "...can have a different kind of bullet."

"You best aim that fucking Spencer elsewhere." Manning came around with one dragoon on the deaduns, the other on Mean George.

Nina smiled, although she was scared shitless. "You might get me, but one of mine's sure to return the favor."

The cleaner one with the cigar elbowed George hard in the shoulder.

He twisted in protest, nearly dropping his rifle. "Ouch, Mase! That fuckin' hurt."

"George, why don't you go see what's keepin' Nancy and Jasmine. See if they been *et*."

"But—"

"Just find them lackadaisies and let me do the fuckin' talkin'! These here are regular folk, and they don't need you gratin' on 'em." A deadun loped out of the shadows and Mason lifted his rifle and ended its existence. He glared at George, who dejectedly kicked at the mud and stomped off.

Mason tipped his hat. "Sorry about that, folks. My name is Mason Daggett, and that was my brother, George."

"Mister Daggett," Pa leveraged himself against one of the axles to stand straighter, taller. It pained Nina to see him having to talk up to another man. "If you and you brother got some kind of ill intent, you best take it on down the way and find yourselves another place to hole up."

Mason looked around. "You call this holed up?"

"Better than nothing. We plan on moving east shortly."

"Look, these afflicted bastards are all over the place. Ain't no safer at the other end of town, what with everything burnin' to the ground. And I see you got your own troubles here. Might be good to stand together." He paused while Manning turned and bashed a deadun's skull. It burst like an overripe melon, its stink swirling in the air. "At least for now."

Pa gave the man a good stare, but Nina knew they had

no choice. They needed those rifles on their side. Who knew what else those fellas had stashed away somewhere?

"Fine," Pa said. "But either one of you lay a hand on my daughter, I'll shoot your nuts off before I kill you."

"Perish the thought. We're Southern gentlemen." Mason Daggett took his pistol out and dumped a couple more deaduns into the mud. "So what should I call you kindly folks?"

Manning dispatched another that got a little too close for comfort. "Why don't we thin the herd and leave introductions for later?"

"Fair enough." Mason put his shoulder against the side of the wagon, dropped two more with his pistol, then craned his neck to peer back the way he'd come, evidently looking for his brother.

Nina went to the rail. She helped Pa stand and reloaded her Colt. "I don't like these fellas," she said low.

He nodded. "We'll keep an eye on 'em."

The pile of corpses was growing into a mangled flesh barricade. The deaduns were forced to go around, between, and over bodies stacked two or three high, arms and legs intertwined in a bloody mess of brains and entrails. It was easy pickings now, but wouldn't be for long. Soon they'd be surrounded.

The fire had crossed the divide and burned on both sides of the street. The heat was becoming almost unbearable on Manning's side. Hard to say how it would feel once they were hemmed in.

Nina banged off two shots when a commotion rolled in behind her. Two half-dressed women in striped stockings pushed a wheelbarrow, one to a handle, and set it down with a clatter. One woman was a busty, wide-eyed blond with tear-streaked mascara stains around her eyes; the other was a long-legged black woman with skin like coffee and cream and hair falling in soft, bushy curls around her face. She had striking, light green eyes, and was possibly the most curious and stunning woman Nina had ever seen. Belts of ammunition were slung over their shoulders. Dirt stained their cheap dresses, and mud covered their boots. Nina caught a whiff of cheap perfume. Not entirely a bad thing compared to what they'd smelled out here.

Mean George was with them.

Nina looked into the wheelbarrow and saw a treasure trove: several boxes of pistol cartridges, a few worn-looking pistols, bottles of whiskey, and at least two other rifles, one a Spencer.

George jerked his thumb back in the direction they'd just come from. "I found 'em stuck in a rut back there. Spilled half our shit."

"Did not!" the blond hollered, her voice penetrating Nina's ears. "You assholes left us. Told you not to leave us—"

George took a step and backhanded her across the face. "Shut the *fuck* up, Nancy. That fuckin' mouth of yours... it's a wonder you did any fuckin' business. Make a man's cock shrivel right up."

Nancy pulled a one-shot pistol from her bodice and pointed it at Mean George. She sniffled. "I *told* you not to fuckin' *hit* me."

"Jesus whore on a hot plate, Nancy," George said, grinning and holding his arms wide in mock submission. "You know it ain't my fault. It's that goddamn clattering voice of yours. Sounds like one of those fancy poodle dogs."

"One more time, George…"

Nina was torn between which one to shoot, but she figured the deaduns would be most ideal for now.

Mason took one of the Spencers out of the wheelbarrow and tossed it to Nina. He threw another rifle to Manning. "Alright, folks, glad you're here and getting along fine. How's about we worry about the ones that *ain't* alive!" He looked at Nina. "You run out of bullets, you pass the magazine to one of these cocksuckin' whores, and they'll hand you a full one right back. Loads in through the stock like this." Mason pulled a long, spring-loaded cylinder out of the stock and raised his eyebrows.

Nina nodded. "Got it."

Manning hefted his rifle. "How much you figure you got?"

"About five or six-hundred rounds. Give or take."

Pa fired a couple rounds and shouted over his shoulder. "If ya'll are done conversin', maybe you could turn your attention to the task at hand?"

They took up positions, forming a wall of lead shot and black powder determination. Five gun barrels pointed west up Main Street, chambers loaded and locked, hammers cocked.

"We draw the line right here," Mason shouted.

"Eat shit, you dead cocksuckers!" George added, taking aim.

Nina and Manning exchanged a look. James shrugged and hefted his weapon.

They fired at will, peppering the shambling forms with bullets, watching them drop into the mud. Nina's ears rang. A black powder cloud got so thick the deaduns became fire-tinged silhouettes in the street. Nina aimed for what she thought were heads, lumps of shadow atop hitching shoulders. She emptied the Spencer, unlatched the magazine from its place in the gun stock, and exchanged magazines with Nancy.

They took down fifty or more of the things in just a few minutes. Bodies littered the street and boardwalks on either side. The fires claimed some, and Nina about gagged on the scents of cooked hair and rancid flesh. A mist of red spray hung in the air from the concussion of lead against skull, mingling with the colored fog, creating a beautiful and terrifying scene, like some mirror image of Hell on Earth. But even with the tremendous firepower, the deaduns still came. Some were even going around the buildings and approaching through side alleys.

"Hold!" Manning shouted.

As the smoke cleared, Nina caught something further back in the deaduns' ranks. A mysterious, non-shambling individual of apparent nefarious intent. At least that's what Nina took from the gestures the thing made; shooing some of the deaduns out and around the defenses, drawing some back, and urging others forward. Some kind of hellish director. She'd bet the thing had full-on black eyes, too.

She remembered that woman who'd come at her speaking words, actual *words*, before Manning put her down. Was some singular intelligence behind all this? Nina sighted on the thing in question and put a bullet through its brain, watching it fall away with grim satisfaction.

"I said, *hold!*"

"Sorry," Nina mumbled.

"It ain't enough," Mason said. "The fire might keep 'em

from flankin' us, but eventually we'll be overrun. We need to get out of here. Any place we can hole up?"

Nina heard a cry from behind her. She twisted to see one of those dead dog things dragging Nancy away through the mud. The blond struggled, screaming, hitting it with her fists, but the mongrel clenched her tight, pulling with uncanny strength. "Help!"

Jasmine hefted a long, heavy pistol and fired, taking off a chunk of Nancy's shoulder. The black girl fired again, ripping through the side of Nancy's throat in a gush of blood. Nancy disappeared, twitching and gurgling, into the fog.

"No! Goddamn it!" Jasmine screamed. She threw the gun down, and sobbed into her hands.

Nina leaned her rifle against the wheelbarrow and put her arm around Jasmine's shoulders. She wasn't sure why, but she felt the need to, and it looked as if nobody else was going to console the poor thing. "Ain't nothing else you could have done." Nina thought it sounded paltry, but what could she say? She had just blown her friend away.

Jasmine looked up through bloodshot eyes. "We... we came on the train together. We never been apart..."

Nina hugged her tight. "You did her a favor. But, we need to keep it together for now. Mourn later. We gotta watch each other's backs, all right?"

An explosion consumed all sound. The ground rocked beneath them, and Nina fell on her ass in a daze wondering what just happened. Her first thought was some powder keg or fuel source had been lit by the raging fire. Then the sky vomited up a gory rain of blood and body parts. An arm hit the side of the wheelbarrow and plopped in the mud. Half a head landed next to Nina with a thud, eyeball oozing out on its bony skull, jaws still connected by a thread of tendon. A bloody chunk of *something* landed in her lap.

A strange croaking sound she'd never made before came from someplace deep in her chest, a sort of horrified revulsion she couldn't quite bodily contain. She turned her head and vomited.

All around shouts of incredulity and surprise rang out above the dull hum in her ears.

"Dadgum 'splosion!"

"Jesus Christ on a fuck-stick!"

"Nina, you alright?"

"Who in Tarnation's *that*?"

"Nina!"

Nina got to her feet and nodded to Pa, even though the world seemed distant and dreamlike. Beyond him, two figures ran toward them down the middle of Main Street. One was a large, healthy-looking man running with long, easy strides. The other was a shorter fellow, scampering crab-like, all hunched over. The two made it to the wagon, and Nina saw why the one man looked so burdened; he carried two large rucksacks packed to the hilt. The weight bore him down, but he didn't seem to mind as evidenced by the shit-faced grin on his powder-blackened face.

Three rifles trained on the newcomers. Hammers cocked in warning.

The larger of the two stepped into the light of the fire. A tall bearded man around Pa's age, Nina figured, looking civilized in his frock coat and fine, flat-brimmed Stetson. The kerchief round his neck had a hint of silk and paisley, which she thought a bit peculiar, then forgot it as the man's tightened gaze measured them, each in turn.

Nina knew the look. When he got to her, she could barely hold his gaze. They stared at one another for a moment before his steely gaze moved on. "Easy, ladies and gents, easy. Just a couple of survivors like yourselves tryin' to make heads or tails of this shitstorm."

"Great," Pa said. "Then you can start by telling us your names, and how much powder you're packin.'"

The man tipped his hat. "I'm James Strobridge, Central Pacific Superintendent. This here is my foreman, Lester Woodruff," he indicated his hunched, thick-bearded companion, who gave them a grubby, wall-eyed stare.

"Call me Woodie," the man said with a rasp, then turned back to admire the flames and smoke behind them.

"We do apologize for the exceptionally loud entrance. Didn't have much of a choice. The gun locker at the rail yard was robbed. Heathens took every damn decent weapon we had."

Pa smiled through his pain and lowered his pistol. "Nice to meet you, Mister Strobridge. I've heard about you." Pa introduced their group, stumbling a bit when he came to Jasmine, still bawling in her hands over her friend's demise. "Looks like you did us a favor, blowin' up those flesh-hungry bastards. Any idea what they are?"

Strobridge shrugged. "We'd just come out of the Canary Hotel and walked straight into this mess. Animals gone bat fuckin' crazy. Horses and dogs eatin' people. Cats doing their damndest to follow suit. People doing god-awful shit to one another. Hotel was overrun before we could get back inside, so we hightailed it down to the rail yard; barely made it. Engineer's office was already ransacked, weapons gone, as well as all my goddamn surveyors and foremen." He smiled. "We'd sure as shit feel much better on the other side of that wagon with you folks."

Pa nodded. "Of course, Mister Strobridge. Come on over. We could probably use you and the dynamite kid there."

Strobridge turned up one corner of his mouth as Woodie fixed a confused look back and forth between his boss and Lincoln.

"That was you who detonated half the town, was it not?" Pa directed the question at Woodie, who still looked back and forth as if waiting for permission to speak.

"Not dynamite," he said, hefting his packs over his rounded shoulders and following Strobridge.

The Daggetts blocked Strobridge and Woodie as they tried to get through. The railroad boss stood straighter, his chest out, looking back and forth between the brothers and grinning like he got a hard-on from fighting just the same as them.

"You're one of them railroad big bugs, huh?" Mean George meant to do his fair share of bullying, Nina reckoned, then she realized she still had one arm around Jasmine and eased herself between the woman and the men squaring off.

"Step aside," Strobridge spoke low, his voice dangerous. "We don't need more difficulty."

He's hoping they won't step aside, though, Nina thought. Strobridge looked like he'd just as soon kill the Daggetts than bother with them another minute. She wasn't sure who was more dangerous.

"Yes sir, Mister Bossman," George said, stepping aside.

"Come on through. Make yourself at home here at the Wagon Wheel Inn. Ya'll need in-room breakfast in the fuckin' mornin'?"

Mason narrowed his eyes, but let them by.

A fresh crowd of deaduns had shuffled in to replace the ones blown to hell; more damn Chinese in their pajama-lookin' clothing, others dressed in dingy rail worker attire, all of them dirt-smeared and bloody, some still carrying pick axes and hammers. Manning stepped up by Nina and fired, then groused across at her pa and the newcomers, "While y'all were chatting our Celestial friends came back for dinner."

The rest of the crew joined in, popping off rounds as casually as they pleased. Nina stood by the wheelbarrow and took out two deaduns creeping in behind. She didn't want to lose Jasmine too, even if she couldn't explain why.

"Shit," she said, as a ponderous group of dead meat lumbered up. These were more intent, pale, white eyes filled with malice. Their mouths moved in a mockery of life, the foul stink of their breath rolling up in a cloud of stench to greet her. Nina pointed her rifle and went from left to right—just like Ma had taught her how to read—blowing seven skulls to bits, pulling out the spent magazine and trading with Jasmine. By the time she lined up the next one, the deaduns were within fifteen feet. Things were closing in, and that familiar tinge of panic grew. Nina wasn't disappointed when Mason Daggett turned to help her, filling the darkening sky with flashes and reports.

Mason shouted, "It's getting thick back here, folks! We're about to be overrun."

George backed up next to his brother and exchanged a

magazine with Jasmine. "We should've already made a run for it, Mason. What the fuck we waitin' fer?"

Nina caught Mason's eye, and she couldn't tell whether or not she liked what she saw. "Now, brother, we help these folks out and maybe get into God's graces. It does appear to be the end of the world, after all."

"We ain't goin' nowhere with that old man hangin' around…"

"Well, you have a point there. I don't see much help for the old man."

Nina suppressed the urge to turn and mow them both down. This was her *pa* they were talkin' about. The one who'd kept her together after Ma was murdered, the one who'd always been…just her pa. On the other hand, she knew they were right.

"Mister Strobridge," Pa shouted in between shots. "You probably know this town better than anyone. Any place we can hole up for a spell while this clears?"

Strobridge leaned against the wagon next to Pa, fingers in his ears. "There's the old abandoned fort down by Maples Creek."

"Fort Bluff?"

"That's the one. You know it?"

"I know of it. Haven't been inside." Pa looked at Nina with those grave eyes of his. "Mister Strobridge, if Mister Woodruff would be kind enough to lend me some of his explosives, whatever they may be, I can hold them here for a little while, give you some time to get away."

Nina stopped shooting. "We ain't leavin' you."

"You've *got* to, Nina. I'm holding you back."

"You heard him, honey," Strobridge said, grabbing a

hunting knife out of the wheelbarrow and flexing it in his hand. Far too practiced for a railroad boss. "Even your pa knows it."

The deaduns encroached, a wall of reaching hands, blackened fingertips grasping at Strobridge's jacket. The railroad boss yelled, kicking one back and put his knife through another's eye socket with a squish. A convergence of gunfire dissolved the deaduns above the neck, heads turning to mush.

Nina's ears hurt so bad she was sure she'd never hear the same again. She was tired and worn down. Mentally exhausted. So, to hell with it—they could say what they wanted, she wasn't leaving Pa. Nina hustled to the wheelbarrow and began rearranging the mess inside, making a relatively comfortable place to sit.

"The hell you doing, half-breed?" Mean George loomed over her.

"We're putting my pa in the wheelbarrow."

"The fuck we are."

"The fuck I am," Nina said, then ignored George and went to her pa, got under his shoulder. She turned to see George's rifle pointed at her.

"What I meant was the fuck you *ain't*."

Manning lined up his barrel with George's head. Mason followed suit, aiming at Manning, and suddenly there was a crosshatch of steel trained inward with Mister Strobridge and Woodie Woodruff in the middle.

"Now, folks," Strobridge said, raising his sooty hands. "It's all downhill once we hit the trail. Put the gentleman in the barrow and let's move."

Nina looked right into the black hollow of Mean

George's Spencer. "You heard the man. It's all downhill, you ingrate fuck."

George's hand tensed, just the slightest squeeze against the stock, and Nina thought a bright flash of light would be the last thing she ever saw.

"Stand down, Georgie," Mason said, edging closer.

George's face twisted up. "Goddamn it, Mase. This half-Injun bitch—"

"I said. Stand. Down." Mason glared, then softened his stare and whispered something to his brother, something that seemed to ease the sumbitch into a state of relative calm.

"Let's get movin' then." George gestured with his rifle at the wheelbarrow.

Nina and Pa started toward it and Manning stepped up to help, taking her father's other arm.

"Easy now, Lincoln," he said.

Nina was relieved for his help and watched her pa get comfortable. He looked downright chagrined but she was dead-set on not leaving behind the only person in the world she loved and who loved her.

"Everybody down! Fire in the hole!" Woodie Woodruff cackled like a madman and tossed a sizzling clay ball into the moaning crowd.

CHAPTER FIVE

Nina's ears rang with the rush of blood, heart hammering inside her chest. Heavy boots pounded against the packed earth and glass clinked as Pa's weight shifted atop the pile of weapons and whiskey. Manning had both wheelbarrow handles, hanging on for all his worth as they careened down the trail at breakneck speed.

The Daggetts had taken the lead, along with Strobridge and Woodie, heads swiveling as their eyes raked every forest shadow. Strobridge held a makeshift torch, just a stick wrapped in an old cloth and doused with whiskey. Nina jogged a little behind, intent on keeping those shifty Daggetts in sight, but that wasn't her only concern; her imagination ran wild in the dark. Hands reached for her from behind every tree trunk, and the swat of sticker

branches against her overalls were fingers grasping at her, teeth fastening tight on her bare skin. She pictured a horde of deaduns around every bend in the trail, weird eyes aglow with that unholy light, mouths agape with that despairing, singular moan.

Nina shook her head, figuring she'd best focus on not falling over something in the dark and busting her ass. Pa depended on her now, and she wouldn't let him down. Her stomach twisted with the thought of losing him, and she was happy with herself for standing up to Mean George, even if she might have risked a bullet in the ol' bean for rubbing him raw. They'd need to keep an eye on that bag of bluster. She was glad Manning seemed to be of the same mind, although she chided herself for the thought. Pa and her had always been more than sufficient, just the two of 'em, and that's how she preferred it. Even so, she welcomed the extra muscle.

And he weren't none too awful to look at either.

Although as far as attraction went, Nina realized her gaze kept returning to Jasmine. The woman's hips were hypnotizing from beneath her plain, loose dress. Nina hadn't thought about it before, had never met many *professional* ladies, but she could see why men paid to have those long, dark arms around them. In any case, Jasmine helped Nina keep her mind off them deaduns, for the moment, leastwise.

But right then a noise reached Nina's ears. She looked around, but no one else seemed to notice. Sounded like the yelp of a dog. Perhaps they hadn't heard, or maybe her imagination was playing more tricks. Then another cry came through the trees, high-pitched, more like a person than a hound that time.

"Wait." Nina caught Jasmine by the shoulder even as the others plowed ahead. "Stop!" she cried. Manning skidded to a halt, nearly spilling Pa. The others crouched, gripping their guns, panting.

"What?" Manning whispered, pulling a dragoon from its holster.

A dog's bark, then the scream again. Nina's heart thumped. Her priority was to get Pa to safety, but damned if it didn't sound like a kid was in trouble somewhere out there, and not too far away she reckoned.

They waited, looking at one another, for half a minute or more.

"Whoever it was, they've stopped," hissed Strobridge. "Let's get mov—"

A man's desperate voice reached them. "No! Rachel!"

Then a woman's wail, followed by that youthful scream again.

"We have to help." Nina grabbed a spare magazine from Jasmine.

"You fuckin' kiddin'? Like hell!" George shook his head.

Mason approached Nina. "No offense, Injun girl, but we got our own problems. What's theirs is theirs."

"Damn right, brother. *Exactly* fuckin' right."

Strobridge took his hat off and put it over his heart. "Sorry for those poor folks, my dear, but they're making enough commotion to draw those things away from us. We'd be remiss not to take advantage of the opportunity."

Nina felt bile rise in her throat. "You call yourselves men?" She shook her head.

Strobridge held up his hands. "Fine, go, but don't go

shooting in the middle of the woods. You'll bring the goddamn monsters down on all our heads."

Nina handed Jasmine her rifle. "Gimme my ax," she said to Manning.

Mason kicked the ground and shook his head. "Damn, you hit low, girl. Jabbing at a man's courage. Guess I'll come, just to keep you from getting' et, but if there's more than a couple of them dead bastards, we shin out. Got it?"

Nina gave a noncommittal grunt. He was lucky to get that much from her.

Manning stepped in close to her. "I'll come, too" he said low.

"I'd be obliged for it, but..." Nina flicked her eyes toward Mean George and that creepy Woodie feller who looked like he'd lost his mind way before this fucked-up day of days.

Manning understood and nodded. "Alright then," he said. "Do what you gotta. Be careful. Mind your step out there, Nina...and holler like the dickens if you need help."

She nodded, then stepped over to Pa and grabbed his hand. "I wish..."

"We been through all kinds of hell, girl. Way before this. Just do as I taught you."

Strobridge had lit another torch and handed it to Nina. "We only got a few of these left, and I don't want to waste any more whiskey. Get your asses back here pronto."

"C'mon, Saint Joan. Let's get this goddamned martyr's affair done with," said Mason, and Nina stepped past him as another yell echoed through the woods.

They hotfooted in the direction of those cries, Nina's torch giving off a stingy half-light. They stumbled over rocks, roots, and dead limbs, any of which could have been a deadun lying in wait. If it weren't for Nina's hard boots, she would have twisted her ankle a half dozen times.

The two broke into a clearing and spotted the cause of the commotion; an axle-broke cart wedged against a tree, its horse gone. A terrified woman stood in the cart, arms around what Nina presumed to be her weeping daughter. A man stood his ground in their defense, wielding a large piece of lumber against at least four deaduns. He wasn't a big man, but fierce all the same, kicking and swinging that ponderous wood, knowing exactly what was at stake.

The nearest deadun was hunched over a lifeless foxhound, gnawing away. Nina dropped her torch, took two steps, and buried her ax in the filthy deadun's skull with a wooden *thunk*. She kicked the body in the back to leverage her ax out, but her hands were slick with sweat and gore and the haft slipped free of her grasp.

A deadun spun on her unexpectedly quick and grabbed her shoulder with one clawed hand. The other knocked her hat off, got a handful of her hair. Nina backed up while her head jerked forward. Her shooting hand closed around the deadun's throat, keeping the monster at arm's length even as it pulled her hair into its mouth and chewed. They wrestled standing up. Nina's neck wrenched. The creature was strong as a damned ox. Might have been a man, but she couldn't be sure in the dark all spun around.

Nina gritted her teeth and twisted her hips, trying for her hunting knife sheathed behind her holster, but the deadun gripped her tight. She kicked out, hoping to knock it off balance. Her boot connected once, twice, a third time; something popped with a sickening crunch, and the deadun went down, taking her with it.

Nina landed hard on one knee, tumbled sideways. Head spinning, bearings lost, not knowing up from down, then moaning and *clack-clacking* loud in her ears, way too close. She sensed the deadun's jaws snapping near her left cheek.

Hand still locked around its throat, she pushed and won a little space. She reached across her body and got her knife, then sawed at her long hair. A dry tearing sound, and then she was free! The deadun still held several inches of her hair in its fist, chewing the dark locks.

Nina's fury became a spike of heat. She lifted her hunting knife and plunged it blindly at the deadun's head, sloughing off pieces of scalp and facial flesh, then puncturing the creature's eye in a gush of phlegm and blood, splitting socket bone to the hilt.

She pulled the blade free and looked up. Mason stood there, wiping his knife on a rag, grinning. The family huddled together, looking from Mason to Nina.

"Thanks for the help." She stood and glared at him.

"Aw now, you look like you had things handled. Loved the way you…" he made a swiping motion, "…chopped your hair off, though Injuns are especially practiced at that."

Nina curled her lip and retrieved her hat and ax while Mason chuckled. To hell with him. Wasichu took as many scalps as the People, she knew for a fact, all for their blam'd paper money. Her perception of Mason Daggett being the more rational of the two brothers was way off—he was just a more shrewd kind of dangerous.

She placed her hat on her head and started for the family when the young girl, maybe twelve-years-old Nina reckoned, broke away from her ma and made for the dead hound. "Bacon!" the girl yelled and leaned over the bloody dog. She broke into a new rash of tears.

"Hey now, you need to stop that ruckus," Mason chided. "You're going to bring more of 'em down on us."

The father approached and put a hand on the sobbing girl. "Shhh, now, Rachel. The man's right."

"C'mon, let's get." Mason turned and stepped off into the darkness.

"Follow us," said Nina.

"Wait. Who are you people?" the man asked.

"No time for that now. Just keep quiet and stay close."

Nina didn't want to be a hard ass. Her heart went out to the terrified girl who gazed at her with eyes the size of the moon, but there weren't nothing she could do right now other than lead them back to the group.

Nina gathered a little about the family, speaking in whispers as they walked. The Buells, they were called; Grover, his wife Clara, and daughter Rachel. Nina asked them where they'd first seen the deaduns.

"*Deaduns*. That's as good a name as I've heard," Grover panted, helping his wife and girl along. The family was having a hell of a time in the faint torchlight, tripping over just about everything and making Nina even more nervous. "They run us out of our shop, just like they done a lot of folk. We were lucky. Had the wagon hitched out back and was just about to head home anyway..." His voice faded as he put his arm around his dazed daughter to move her along. Clara walked behind them, her eyes darting everywhere.

Mason paused and shushed them, and Nina thought it best not to ask any more questions. Get everyone to safety and hash out the rest then. There were still other assholes to deal with, *living* ones.

"There's Bossman's torch," Mason pointed ahead, and after a moment Nina picked it out. A tiny flicker in the pitch black. They made a direct line to that spot, stumbling back on the trail.

Pa's face lit up when he saw Nina. He grinned and squinted up at her. "You okay?"

Nina rubbed her neck and smiled. "Got jerked around a little, but we managed to help these folks out."

"Great," said George. "More mouths to feed."

Nina scowled. "You know, you spew a lotta fuckin—"

"No, no please, it's alright," Grover responded. "We'll hold our own." The man wrapped his arms around his wife and daughter.

"Undoubtedly," Strobridge said. "Now let's get moving, people."

"Where are you folks bound?" Grover asked.

"Fort Bluff," Pa answered.

"Well that fort's abandoned. No one's been stationed there for a couple years. No one's there to protect us."

"Why don't ya'll just wander on back wherever the fuck you came from then, hmm?" Mean George said, then spat and walked off after Mister Strobridge, Woodie, and his brother.

Grover exchanged a look with his wife, then nodded. "Beggars ought not to be choosers."

"Pappy, I just want to go home," said his daughter.

"I know, pretty girl, but it's best we stay in a group."

"Your pa's right," said Nina's father. "Right now our only strength is in numbers."

"Are you…have you been bit?" Clara Buell asked Pa.

"No, ma'am. My foot's busted pretty good and James here enjoys playing pack mule."

Manning hefted up the back end of the wheelbarrow. "Speaking of, let's shin out. Bossman and the Scalawag Brothers don't seem to be slowing the pace none."

They headed off and the trail soon steepened in that soulless darkness, causing Nina to move in front of the wheelbarrow and hold it steady to keep it and Pa from wrecking. Manning seemed a right fit fellow, but he was still grunting and clenching his jaw, though neither he nor anyone else complained, despite the slow progress. Bone-weariness had taken them all, as well as a dull stupor; their world, or at least this part of it, had changed out of the blue and in one hell of a way.

What would her mother have thought about all this? No doubt she would've faced east, sweeping her arms wide and uttering her usual Shoshoni wisdom, a prayer song to Duma Appah, something Nina would never understand. A sudden pressure formed behind her eyes, and tears burned them. No! She wouldn't think about her ma, although Nina feared she needed her memory more than ever right now.

The ground leveled out somewhat, and Pa said, "James, you need a break?"

"I'm fine."

Nina caught a glimpse of Manning in the faint moonlight and saw his face shined with sweat. She thought about speaking up, but then her pa continued, "Alright, well, ain't much further, if you're sure, and all."

"I can help," Grover Buell offered.

"I'm fine, thank you," Manning said again.

"All right, well, if you do need a break for a minute…"

Manning nodded and smiled and kept pushing.

They followed the overgrown dirt track out into the open toward a massive shadow squatting in the darkness. The sound of trickling water reached Nina's ears.

"Maples Creek," Pa said.

Although she and Pa had never been this way, they had a few decent maps of the surrounds, and from what she remembered, the abandoned Fort Bluff sat upon a rise less than a quarter mile south of the creek.

"How's your foot, Pa?"

He shook his head, giving her a stare she felt through the darkness. He was right. Wouldn't do any good discussing his injury—his *weakness*—in front of the others. Bad enough he had to rely on a stranger to wheel him over rough terrain. It had to stick right deep in her father's craw they'd been forced to rely on a stranger's good will. The way she reckoned it, though, without James Manning she and her pa would have never left Coburn Station alive. Or at least not alive in the way they were at present.

A couple minutes later, Nina made out a jagged line against the clouds; a wall of sharpened wood logs pointing at the sky. There were gaps in the line, entire sections fallen away from disrepair. Strobridge lit another torch and more of the wall was revealed. Made of old timber, moss-covered and rotted, it looked like you could poke a stick right through.

"This wall's a piece of *shit*," George notified everyone of the obvious.

"That's why we're going in, brother."

"Shh," someone whispered.

Strobridge shuffled along, hand up, his voice an urgent whisper. "Now, I toured this place years back when Cap'n Stewart and Colonel Hays was skirmishin' those fuckin' Injuns from Truckee down to Pyramid Lake, and if memory serves, some of the buildings inside are adobe and may still be sound."

Pa cleared his throat. "Fort like this probably got a hospital inside. Likely be the most solid structure aside from the ammunition depot and officers' quarters. These kinds ain't built so much for defense, but to establish a presence and offer aid to local settlers and trappers and the like."

Mason's face was shadowy amusement. "How you know all that, old man?"

"I been running scout missions through these territories since before you were born, *boy*. I seen every type of fort ever made, and I know how the men who build 'em think."

George leaned over Pa. "Looks like we got us a gin-u-wine Injun scout." He leered at Nina before looking back at her pa. "Why don't you show us more of what you learnt, maybe one of them rain dances? Oh, damn. I forgot. You got a gimp fuckin' foot."

"Back off," Nina warned.

"Or *what*, half-breed?"

Nina's instinct was to lash out, but a spike of fear crippled her anger. Pa was immobile, *vulnerable*, and she couldn't afford to make a wrong decision now. Not with these Daggett assholes so heavily armed. There were the Buells and Jasmine, too. Nina would have to play it safe, have to take some responsibility; difficult given Pa had always been that force in her life. In any case, George

Daggett was no doubt her enemy. Nina remained silent, patting Pa on his shoulder and offering to help Manning with one of the wheelbarrow handles.

Manning shook his head. "I am right as rain," he said, but she noticed his gaze never left Mean George, who smirked and spat, then turned his attention back to the dilapidated fort wall.

At the fort entrance, the thick wooden doors hung open in the flickering torchlight. Shadows capered in the parade ground beyond. Everything smelled old and moldy, dead. Nina thought going inside was somehow the best *and* worst possible idea imaginable.

Moans echoed down from the forest around them, hollow things from soulless creatures hidden in the darkness. The sound was akin to wolves howling, only made up of human voices, colder and even hungrier. Chills shook Nina's shoulders.

"Probably all through the damn hills." Strobridge looked around, eyes narrow and sharp.

"I'm certain they are," agreed Grover Buell.

"Then our torches must look like dern beacons to them," Pa said. "Hard to tell how good they can see."

"Are you shittin' me?" George pointed up into the surrounding hills. "We're ringin' the dinner bell, and they ain't havin' furry fuckin' forest creatures neither. It's *us*."

"I agree," said Mason. "No telling what's inside, but we sure as hell know what's outside."

They went through the gates and entered the wide, grassy parade ground. Long, partially collapsed structures lay to their left and right. Probably stables or barracks, Nina figured. Ahead across the expanse were smaller buildings tumbled sideways and falling apart in big piles of crumbled brick and rotting wood. Something massive sat behind the mess, something Nina hoped was their salvation.

"Look. There's a light," Woodie said, his arm poking out from beneath his load of rucksacks and weathered baggage.

"Hmmm, I believe you're right," Strobridge squinted. "What say you Daggett boys go have a look for us?"

"Fuck you, mister. Have your own goddamn look."

"Now, pull your horns in, Georgie," his brother said. "Let's find out what it's worth to the big Bossman."

Strobridge's grin lit up, looking evil in the golden glow. "Thirty dimes a piece. That worth a quick peek?"

Mason nodded to George. "You bought yourself a couple scouts, Bossman."

"He ain't no skin-flint," Mean George said. "Half up front."

Strobridge chuckled and reached into his coat, procured a small leather pouch, and shook it, rendering the unmistakable clink of coins. "Payment in full once services are rendered, boys. Take it or leave it."

Mason whacked his brother on the arm. "C'mon."

"Ow!" George grumbled, then the two moved off into the darkness.

Nina groaned low in her throat as they wandered off. It wasn't just the Daggetts she had to worry 'bout.

"You okay?" Manning said low, bumping Nina with his elbow as he stretched his arms. Nina couldn't see his expression, but his tone held a warmth usually reserved for kin or persons of *special* interest. Might James be sweet on her in all this accursed mess? Made sense, she supposed, why he'd go to such lengths as he had, being a practical stranger and all.

"I'm fine." Nina shook her head, considered her father still sitting in the wheelbarrow. "We need to take a look at that foot as soon as we can."

"We got other things to worry about," her pa said with a stubborn frown, but she could tell he knew she was right, and he had no good reason to protest. They needed to get that boot off, and *soon*. His foot might heal poorly if not set right. A broken foot, even a twisted ankle, could hobble a man the rest of his life.

They packed together, aware of the cold after having come to a stop. The Buells stood in back, pressing in on Jasmine, who pressed in on Manning and Nina. Normally, Nina would have an aversion to the proximity of so many others. Her pa had preached awareness of the space around her, but at the moment Nina didn't mind the closeness one bit.

Funny how things affected complete strangers.

The young girl, Rachel, sniffed and shivered against her mother's skirts. Grover held his wife's shoulders and peered around nervously. Nina silently wished the best for them, but a hard world had just gotten a thousand times harder.

"Psst," hissed Mason Daggett from the shadows. "It's us. Don't shoot."

Strobridge leaned forward, cupped his hands over his mouth, and whispered. "What did you find?"

The brothers jogged up. Mason pointed back to the ruins and used the tip of his finger to relay specifics. "Past those broke buildings is a sturdy one of clay brick, big, defensible. There's other entrances, too, around the sides and back. We tried a couple of them. Boarded up or locked.

There's something else." He looked askance at George.

"Well? What is it?"

"There's definitely people inside. And the deaduns agree, because there's about a dozen of those shuffling goners all 'round the main entrance."

"Shit."

"Shit's right… but we can take 'em."

"You volunteering?"

"Yeah, I'm volunteering *everyone*."

CHAPTER SIX

Nina thought the raiding party, for that's what they'd become, was likely a poor match for the mass of clawing, snarling deaduns at the door, but she had to admit getting some rest behind a solid wall sounded more than a little appealing.

It was worth the risk. *Had* to be. Manning gave Nina's shoulder a reassuring squeeze. She smiled back even though his touch wasn't all that comforting. His grip was cold and hard.

Mason quickly whispered his plan, got nods from Strobridge and Pa, and they were suddenly out in the open, fanning out like assassins. Only Clara and Rachel remained behind with Pa, none of them able carry on a proper fight. Hell, Nina wasn't even sure about Grover or

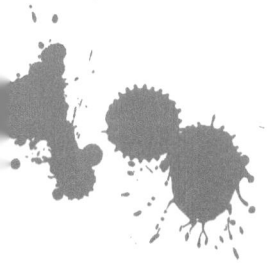

Jasmine, but they'd have to find their balls sooner rather than later because the world wasn't gonna hold their damn hands.

Nina picked out her target, a tall, thick fellow, arms up and groping across the wall in stupid exploration. She glued her eyes to the base of the deadun's neck, intent on burying her blade there. And then she made the mistake of glancing at Jasmine. The woman was all but petrified, holding the blade she'd been given like it was a glowing-hot horseshoe. The woman had probably never sliced a potato much less driven a blade through muscle and bone.

Nina quickened her pace. She needed to take hers out in time to help Jasmine before she got herself killed. Someone hissed at her to slow down, but she was already there, plunging her knife into the deadun's neck. At least that's how she'd imagined it. Reality had its own ideas.

Her overhand swing was strong, just like gutting a strung-up hog, but the blade hit skull and turned downward. Nina pushed with her forearm across its back, pinning the thing against the wall as she pulled her knife free and got ready to take another whack at it, but the deadun spun, his flattened face resembling an angry shovel, and knocked her aside with ease.

Right into another. Damned if there weren't two of'em now, with her trapped between 'em. The one behind her got its wiry hands wrapped around her neck. She was in a heap-full now.

Something snatched her hat off her head. She heard a throaty growl. Wet struck her nape. Cold, foul breath tickled her skin. She flinched, but swallowed her panic. Pa had taught her a thing or two about fighting off sneak attacks.

She dropped quick, slipped from the grasp of the deadun at her back, and went down on one knee. Just as she broke free, something slammed into the corpse behind her, sent it flinging over her shoulder into ol' shovel-head. The two flesh-hungry growlers groped and stumbled around one another in a macabre dance.

"Here!" Jasmine extended her arm. Nina took her hand and let herself be pulled to her feet, got her bearings, and shimmied in for another strike. If she missed again...

The deadun that had grabbed hold of her neck a second ago was a few inches shorter, with a tangled mop of dirty blond hair. Nina flipped her blade point-up and moved in. Blondie got herself turned around, searching for lost prey, but Nina was on her, grabbed a handful of hair and plunged her knife into the snarling woman's temple, easy as butter. The deadun dropped like a rock.

Then shovel-head was on her, more hell-fired than ever, making guttural, feral noises.

Jasmine found her courage...and her voice. Leading with a yell, she dashed up and started beating shovel-head with fist and blade, a whirlwind of knuckles and steel. Nina stepped back to avoid Jasmine's wild swings as much as the deadun's gnashing teeth. Despite the woman's ferocity, shovel-head was hardly deterred. It batted at Jasmine's arms, grabbed at the knife, pushed and battled the raging woman to a standstill.

Nina knew Jasmine would be tuckered out in a matter of seconds. And, unfortunately, it didn't appear these deaduns ever tired. Nina went to the wall, nearly tripping on the woman she'd just put down, and moved in from behind. Her options were break its knee, grab its shirt and pull it to the ground, or attempt another quick stab to the brain.

It. She'd been thinking of the dead man—the *undead* man—as an it. Damn. These poor souls didn't choose to be this way, but...*hell, it's us or them. Us or them.*

Nina meant to survive long as she could.

With that in mind, something knocked her to the ground and she found herself beneath a pile of grunting bodies. An elbow connected with her head. The world spun. A wave of nausea started in her stomach, threatening to eject what little was left in it. On instinct, she swung her fists and kicked her feet, half-crawling, fully expecting the pressure and sharp pain of a deadun's teeth on her leg. Someone yowled, weight shifted, and she crawled free.

The scene was chaos. Across the front of the building silhouettes danced death to a damnable beat. Jasmine was bent near backward keeping shovel-head at arm's length as he tried to gnaw her face off. The woman's terrified gaze tugged at Nina, and she raised her fist to rush in and stab the deadun.

That's when a cloaked figure strode out of the darkness. The man's face was shrouded in shadow beneath the brim of his hat but for a dark beard. Nina caught a flash of white collar.

The stranger approached, placed his hand on shovel-head's shoulder, and said, "By the Grace of God and Saint Ignatius, I expel thee from the Devil's yoke."

Nina's jaw must have dropped when the growling deadun seized up. Its back jerked straight, hands clenching into claws. Smoke curled up from the man's fingertips where he touched the foul thing.

"Rwwreeee!" the deadun squealed, collapsing as if headshot, never to move again.

The stranger caught Jasmine before she hit dirt. His shadowed face turned to Nina. "Are you unharmed, sister?"

She wasn't sure just how to respond, and a nearby struggle stole her attention; the same pile she'd just crawled out from.

"Goddammit," sputtered George Daggett, trapped beneath a deadun, grappling for his life, face twisted in a grimace with his bared teeth visible even in this merciless dark. For a moment, she debated leaving him there, but surprised herself by taking a handful of the thing's hair and giving it the same treatment with her hunting knife she'd given blondie. Nina let it collapse on top of George.

The others milled around in various states of disarray. Apparently, everyone had made it, no one had gotten bit, which was pretty dern miraculous; Grover and Clara had even managed to wheel Pa up.

The black-robed stranger waved his hands for everyone to gather. "Listen now, brothers and sisters. More of the... *unfortunates* will be coming down from the hills so, if you would, please come with me." To Nina, the man's voice exuded an exaggerated calm with a tinge of mystic inflection, a sort of goodly importance, and a hint of something holy beyond words.

Mason Daggett, breathing heavily, was not impressed. "And who the fuck are you?"

"Easy now. Don't you see? This man is a Black Robe," said Strobridge, brushing at his sleeve. "Everyone, this is Father Thomas Mathias of the Society of the Lord Jesus Christ."

The man stared at Strobridge for a long, odd second.

"You are all welcome here," he said, then looked at both Daggetts, "but I respectfully beseech you not to blaspheme God's name in my company."

George opened his mouth to likely do just that, but his brother chimed in first. "So, there an easier way in?" Mason asked, tightening the reins on his curt tone.

"Easier, yes, if you come in peace. Much harder if you have...*other* intentions. We could, of course, use your help fixing up the place."

"We'll respect your wishes, Father. Lead on," Pa said, and that seemed to settle it.

"Very well, let us make haste. This way."

Manning took the wheelbarrow's handles from the Buells with a nod, and they followed this Black Robe fellow past a set of double doors and more boarded-up windows, and then around the short side to the back. Nina watched the priest, trying to puzzle him out. She didn't know much about the Black Robes, but whatever the man had done to that deadun spooked her about as much as the deaduns themselves.

Mathias knocked on the door and called out, "It's me!"

Nina heard the sounds of objects being moved, and the doors scraped open, loosing the warm glow of lantern light from within.

"Don't be afraid, friends. Everyone here's on the side of the living," the priest said, entering the room and gesturing for them to follow. "This large fellow here is Deputy Marshal Samuel Oden. He speaks softly, but carries a big stick."

The tall, blond man tipped his dark hat and gave the party a nod. The man stood well over six-and-a-half-feet tall, with a barrel chest beneath his long coat and stained denim shirt and a jaw that looked carved from an oak tree.

Mathias smiled and patted another fellow on the back. "And this ruffian here is Buck Patterson. He may look frightful, but he knows the Lord well."

"I attended mass once if that's what you mean, Father." Buck's voice was a growl of pickax over gravel. He was smaller than Marshal Oden—well, they all were—and as wiry and screw-faced as Mean George, but with a heap of rugged ranger thrown in to boot.

With his shaggy mustache, greasy shoulder-length hair, and fringed rawhide jacket, Buck was certainly a rough character, Nina agreed, but he didn't put off a bastardly streak like the Daggett brothers. She got a good feeling from the marshal, too. Something honest about the lines on his weathered face.

The rest of the group had gathered inside, seemingly glad to have four solid walls around them. Whatever this place had been, hardly a remnant remained. Based on what Nina had seen outside, and where she stood now, the structure appeared to be three large rooms—they stood in the center one—with a fourth smaller room, connected to the main facility by way of an enclosed passage. Nina's eyes searched the darkness, but aside from a low-burning lantern sitting on an old barrel, there was no light. Just enough to see by but not *be* seen. Smart.

Movement caught Nina's eye. Strobridge pulled Woodie with him off into the right-hand room. *What were those two up to?*

Mathias continued, "We do have two more fellows here. Hard workers. One is a good friend of Buck's..."

A figure stepped into the lantern light on Nina's left,

sending the Buells into a screeching panic. Grover pushed Clara and Rachel to the side, keeping himself between the newcomer and his family.

A native tribesman in a blood-spattered vest and beads around his neck confronted them. His complexion was at least five shades darker than Nina's, his hair long and sleek like black silk and ornamented with a long feather. She didn't mark him as hailing from her mother's tribe, the Shoshone. No, his adornments gave him away as Paiute, Bannock, or Nez Perce perhaps.

The Daggetts drew their side arms and moved to shield the Buells, not so much to protect them, Nina thought, but to find a better angle to shoot from. The native took a step back, his eyes still cool, as if he'd been in a thousand similar situations.

Buck Patterson drew on the Daggetts. His weapon was the biggest, ugliest black revolver Nina had ever seen. Barrel had to be a mite larger than forty-four caliber. Hell the damn thing looked like a cannon; a *decorated* cannon with red and white feathers dangling from the stock.

Even George Daggett glanced down the barrel and gulped.

Mathias held up his hands and got between the two groups. "True, this man is a native of these lands, but you can rest assured he means no harm. Red Thunder is converted, *friends*, only wishing to—"

"Only good Injun is a dead one, and that's a goddamn fact." George cocked his weapon.

"That's right," Mason said. "I say we send him up to God and let *Him* decide."

It wasn't a difficult decision to make. Nina hated the

Daggetts in just about every way imaginable, so she drew her Colt and pointed it right at Mean George's thick head. She didn't want to see this Red Thunder hurt, but she secretly wished for an excuse to pull the trigger.

Manning aimed his dragoons, one at each brother.

"Fuckin' figures," George said, glancing at the array of weaponry aimed in their direction.

A grin pulled at Nina's lips but she curbed it quick-like. James Manning *was* sweet on her.

"Now, boys," Pa said. "Not every Indian is a devil."

"You would say that, seeing as you got an Injun daugh—"

Pa started to rise up out of the wheelbarrow, and Mason switched his target to cover him.

"Don't be stupid," said Manning, his tone low and nerveless.

"Or what?"

"Or what?" Manning raised a brow. "Look around. Five barrels, one of them a big fucking barrel, versus your two."

Pa held up his hands. "Lord knows I understand how you boys feel. I fought my share of natives in my time, as well as Rebs like yourselves. No, don't deny it. I see it in you. You got Confederate balls, but you're surly as hell, too. Pissed off the war didn't go your way. But it don't matter none now. We all got a common enemy." Pa pointed around. "Those deaduns out there. They don't care a Continental whether you're Indian, graycoat, or an old dried-up pecker like me."

George Daggett snickered, but he wasn't pacified in the least. "Fuck it! Those things out there gonna get us anyway. Might as well take a couple redskins with us."

Manning cocked his dragoons. "You can try."

Tension pushed down like lead clouds. For a moment, Nina didn't think they would ever break, but a sudden chorus of discordant moans assaulted them from outside the open doors. Rachel Buell whimpered.

"No. The old man is right," Mason said, uncocking and lowering his weapon. "We need every fighting man we got right now. I won't have a problem provided that Injun and his buddy stay on that side yonder, and we'll stay over here."

Manning stood down, Nina reluctantly holstered her weapon. Buck put away his monster revolver. The tension unraveled, and the Daggetts, Marshal Oden, and Manning went to get the two back doors shut and shored up. Just in the nick of time, too. Soon as they slid the bar in place, the wet slap of fists pounded against the wood. The door was thick, not nearly as rotten as everything else. Seemed it would hold for a time. The men shoved an old three-legged table in front of it for good measure.

Marshal Oden said, "The room you Daggett boys are in needs two windows repaired, and there's a three-inch crack in one of the corners."

"Figures." George spat.

"Let's go see," Mason said, slapping his brother on the shoulder.

Oden narrowed his eyes at them a little. "There's some old wooden crates over here," he said as they sauntered off. "We'll grab what we can and do some shoring up. Oh, and keep an eye upward."

Nina looked up and saw what the marshal meant. Part of the wood-shingled roof had collapsed, leaving them exposed to the night sky. Not a danger at the moment, but if those things learned to climb...

"Deputy marshal, huh?" Manning asked. "Where outta?"

"Laramie."

"What are you doing way out here in the Sierra Nevadas?"

The two men grabbed hold of another old broken table and moved it together as the marshal continued, "Thomas and I go back a couple years, and he asked for an escort west. Got two brothers handling things for me until I get back."

"If they're as big as you I imagine Laramie's in capable hands."

They wedged the table against the back doors next to the three-legged one.

The marshal put his large hand on the door as deaduns pushed and scratched on the other side of it. "Being big has advantages…Mister Manning, is it?"

Manning nodded and Nina, being perceptive, noticed his Adam's apple bob, like he was suddenly troubled.

"Disadvantages, too," Oden said. "Bigger man, bigger target." The marshal grabbed a crate in each hand and headed off to help the Daggetts secure their area.

"Making nice with the law?" Nina asked Manning.

He looked at her and let a couple seconds tick by. "Just being neighborly." He grabbed a couple crates from the pile and followed after the marshal.

More deaduns pounded on the windows and doors, and fists thudded on the stone walls. They were growing in numbers, somehow having followed the group down out of the hills. *But how so quickly?* Perhaps there was a settlement nearby? Perhaps their moans had brought others. Maybe something else? Nina thought about those black-eyed deaduns, different than their soulless brethren. Not that the black-eyes had souls...

Father Mathias didn't seem as fearful of the horde outside. He stepped nearer to Nina and looked up through the gap in the ceiling, his eyes wandering, face peaceful with a gentle smile. "And so we build this house of refuge in the name of the Lord amidst great turmoil in our hearts and minds. We face the demons, even as they seek to drag our souls down into the bowels of Hell. We will prevail, oh yes we will."

"Hey, Father," Mason said, having approached for another wooden crate. "Ease up on the demon talk, would ya?"

Mathias peered past Mason Daggett and his serene expression vanished. "Mister Strobridge. I didn't think to see you again so soon."

Strobridge had his hands on his hips, surveying rather than pitching in to help the others. "I didn't think to see you again ever. I certainly never thought you'd have the balls to come back here, Thomas."

The priest recovered, his peaceful aspect returning. "I couldn't very well let you get away with blind thievery."

"A fair deal is what it was." Strobridge approached and stood square just a few feet away. Nina backed up a step, feeling the tension between the men. She saw Woodie standing back against the wall, clinging to the shadows but watching with interest.

"I'd hardly call it that," said the priest. "But we can agree to disagree...for now."

Marshal Oden returned and stopped, keen-eyed. "You two know each other?" He stepped between them.

Strobridge's face became an expression of condescending amusement. "Oh, Thomas and I have parleyed back and forth on a couple things."

"Back and forth. A funny way of putting it. Seems to be a one-way street with you, Mister Strobridge."

"I guess we've got a problem to work out then."

Mathias nodded. "Yes, Mister Strobridge. We do."

"I'll meet you in the middle once we get situated. If we're not dead."

Mathias nodded again. "Fair enough."

Strobridge nodded at Mathias, again at the marshal, then gave Nina a wink.

She imparted a frown, and he gave a wry smile before turning and rejoining Woodie.

"Strobridge," Marshal Oden said to himself, then looked at the priest. "J.H. Strobridge, that's the railroad bug you told me about. The one who—"

"Yes, Marshal. That's the one."

Nina bit her tongue, wanting like hell to indulge her curiosity. Instead she fixed on James Manning, who walked by and spared her a quick look as he accompanied Buck Patterson now into the room opposite the Daggetts and Buells, discussing some weak points in the building and how to fix them. Nina was glad the Daggetts called the other room. She didn't think she could stand dealing with the deaduns *and* George Daggett another second. If given a choice, she might well choose the dead folk. With all the tension in this place, the living were right obnoxious.

The only ones she felt truly sorry for were the Buells. And Jasmine.

The prostitute stood arms crossed, looking as helpless

as she likely felt. Nina walked over to her, saw her once pretty dress was covered in muck and blood and she was shivering so hard Nina could practically feel her vibrations. On instinct, she reached out and put a hand on the woman's arm. Jasmine's skin was cold beneath her fingers. The woman looked at Nina's hand, then at Nina and swallowed.

"Hey," Nina whispered.

"I want to thank you, Miss."

"Pfft, I ain't no miss."

"Then that makes two of us." They gazed at one another, then Jasmine flashed a smile and her face prettified despite the soot and blood smeared across her dark features.

Nina returned her smile. It felt like a genuine moment and she felt a feminine affinity she rarely had occasion to enjoy. "We need to get you warmed up—"

Someone cleared their throat. Both of them laid eyes on Mean George, who made a *come here* gesture with his fingers. "You're with us."

Jasmine's gaze cut across the room and back to Nina. The smile faded, and she started over to George. Nina hadn't let go of her arm and she squeezed it with more force than she intended, causing Jasmine to look down at her hand.

"You ain't gotta do nothing he says."

George clicked his tongue. "We done paid for her."

"In case you ain't noticed, a few things have changed since then."

"Ownin' pussy never changes, come hell or high water." George smiled. "Damn, Injun girl. You in love or somethin'? Don't worry, we'll take good care of her. Won't wear that hole out too much."

Jasmine slid her arm from Nina's grip. "It's okay, luv. I dealt with worse."

Nina watched her go. She sniffed and bit her bottom lip, then walked back to her pa.

"You okay, Nina girl?"

"Fine. Other than us being stuck in this goddamn nightmare."

"Just keep it together. You and me, we'll find a way out of all this. We just need a little respite for a few hours, then—"

"Pa. The dead are rising and walking around sinking their goddamn teeth in the living like we ain't ought but vittles. They're everywhere. There ain't no place safe. And here we are like rats, holed up with more bad men, the kind we've been avoiding or fighting the past ten goddamn years."

"Nina, your language—"

"My language? Pa, you're gonna chastise me for cussing during this shitstorm?"

"You're tired. I'm tired. But always have respect for the Lord. I thought I—"

"Your Lord, not mine."

"Nina…"

"No," she put up her hand. She got behind the wheelbarrow and lifted. Pa wasn't a big man, but he weren't all that light either. Her shoulders and neck ached, but her anger gave her strength as she wheeled her father toward the other room. She was done talking for now, and so was he, it seemed.

Their side was a large space with a double door—the very one they'd just fought outside of—and an assortment of chairs and old crates. There was a thin, sagging, wood-framed entrance to the fourth room along the east wall.

Nina passed Red Thunder, who sat cross-legged on the dusty floor, cleaning a pistol. She held his gaze as he looked up, and she swore a hint of smile played across his lips.

Then that goddamn George Daggett called from behind. "Oh no, Injun girl. We done brought that and everything inside it, too." She turned and George stood in the archway. He pointed at the wheelbarrow. "You used it long enough. Get your old man out."

Nina glared at George for a long moment until Manning came walking up behind him, shouldering by and knocked the Daggett forward a step.

"Hey!" George glared at him.

Manning kept on walking. He leaned forward, helping Nina get her father up and out. Pa grimaced as they moved him to the far corner of the room, helped him sit in one of the chairs, and prop his foot up on a crate.

As soon as Pa had sat, they turned to see Buck Patterson give the wheelbarrow a hard push past George and out of the room. "That's fine," he said, and spit a stream of tobacco juice on the ground at George's boots. The Daggett danced back a step and shouted a few choice words.

Buck gave a grin, or maybe it was a scowl. "You have your wheelbarrow. We got the well."

CHAPTER SEVEN

Nina knelt down on the floor in the friendlier section of the building—*their* side—dousing her face with water, rubbing dirt and blood away. It was still cold, the water even colder, but she reveled in it. She took off her hat and ran her hand through her hacked up hair, splashing water into it, wishing she could wipe the whole night away as easily as the dirt.

Buck had been right about the well. A side passage branched off their room, leading east down into another, smaller room, graced with a well that probably tapped into an underwater stream feeding Maples Creek. The roughrider had gone down the well passage and returned grinning ear-to-ear with a sloshing bucket of fresh water.

She and Manning and Pa drunk their fill before dousing themselves, eager to get rid of the stench of blood and filth.

Nina couldn't tell what the other gang was doing across the way—she'd mentally begun calling the Daggetts' side 'Over There'—but there were only four living souls in that group she cared about anyway. The rest could rot in Hell as far as she was concerned.

The deaduns continued to pound away on the outside, mumbling feverishly, moaning and groaning into every crack they could find, driven by some mad hunger Nina could not fathom. Earlier an arm had pressed through a gap between the stone and wooden door frame. Red Thunder's tomahawk had made quick work of the limb.

Another had pushed the stacked crates away from the window and gotten halfway through before Buck and Manning could knife the biter in the head and shove it back out. Even with every weak spot covered, predicting where the next intrusion of dead flesh would occur was the same as shooting craps. They were everywhere.

Nina started to scoop out more water when the marshal yelled from the center room, a place Nina had deemed 'No Man's Land.' "Little help in here!"

"I'll go," Nina told them and scurried to the big man's side.

The room had two sets of double doors, braced by wood and stone and whatever else they could find. Oden leaned against the doors Nina's group had entered by, his powerful frame providing a formidable presence.

It must have been a mass of deaduns pressing in. Nina threw herself against the overstrained barrier, but her weight seemed to make little difference. Wood creaked and Marshal Oden grunted, shoulder and face pressed against the door. The stench of his sweat poured out of the thick coat he wore, his breath hissing between his teeth as he dug in. Standing next to him, Nina realized just what a giant he was.

Father Mathias lent his shoulder, squeezing between Nina and Oden. His boots slipped on the hard-packed ground, forcing him to do a strange sliding walk on the floor.

"We ain't holdin' this, Father." Nina felt around on the wood with her hand. She found a knothole with her finger and drew her Colt, stuck the barrel inside, and popped off three rounds.

"Save your bullets." The priest smiled and winked. "Lead is a worthless substitute for the power of the Lord." He placed his hand against the wood and closed his eyes. The priest's lips moved in a whisper.

Nina strained to hear, drawn in by some mysterious power in his tone. She could not say she had faith in a Supreme Being even though the *wáashat*—the Prophet Dance—of her people during the time of Seven Drums had profoundly moved her as a girl. And she, too, had watched the men of the Goshute do the Sun Dance. Pa even sometimes got Bible-bit after they wintered among the white settlers in the Wind River Mountains or up north on the Feather River, but she'd never heard such devotion come from a white man's lips. Mathias's voice raised, his tone brave yet humble: "While we are unworthy of you, my Lord, protect your faithful as we defend this bastion against those who would defile your name. Take mercy on us, and deliver us into your glory."

A shock ran through the wood, a sort of prickly buzz Nina felt in her hands and face. The hairs on the back of her neck stood up. Nina smiled despite herself, the buzz lightening her heart somehow, the burden of surviving this life, *today*, lifted from her shoulders.

An intensity took hold of Mathias. "Take now the pain from your once loyal, loving flock, and guide their souls to your bosom." His eyes went wide, his jaw clamping shut. Through clenched teeth, he cried out. "And destroy the demon infection that threatens the sanctity of your world! In the name of Jesus Christ, our Savior...*amen!*"

The suffering moans from outside compressed, twisting into high wails, as if the deaduns were being squeezed of whatever demonic life burned within them. Another powerful shock ripped through the wood. Sharp cracks reached Nina's ears. A puff of ghastly smoke entered through the hole Nina had just shot through, the acrid-tinged smell of burnt hair and flesh stinging her nose.

The pressure on the door abruptly ceased, and Marshal Oden turned his back to the barrier and sunk to the floor. Father Mathias rubbed his hand across his face, haggard, his skin sallow, yet he looked at Nina and his eyes still danced with amusement. She couldn't understand why. Nothing amusing about what had just happened, even though they'd won a few more minutes of life. Still, on a night consumed by evil, she was moved by his piety.

"I'm not sure what you did, Father, but that's some powerful stuff."

"It's the Lord's power, not mine," Mathias said, wiping his sweaty brow, then he, too, collapsed down by Marshal Oden on the floor.

Nina stepped away, inspired yet frightened. She wondered about her own faith. Did she even *have* any? She seemed to have lost touch with religion after the death of her mother. How about now, after witnessing this walking evil and Father Mathias's godly power?

Manning brushed past her without a glance, intent on something. "What in the hells do you think you're doing?" he said, tension in his voice.

Nina turned to see who'd drawn Manning's anger. Woodie crouched nearby, two round clay things hanging from his neck, another in his hand. Strobridge was next to him and handed his foreman a torch and stepped back, while the Daggetts and Buells had emerged from their respective areas to look on.

Woodie's wide-set eyes searched overhead, settling on the big gap square in the middle of the roof.

"What are those things?" Manning asked, and Nina saw the clay orbs had fuses attached.

"We're going to clear a few of these bastards out," Strobridge said.

"Clear them...you mean, that's powder, ain't it?"

"Black powder's the stabilizer," Woodie said absently, still looking up. "Howden's concoction. One part powder to two parts *kieselguhr*, add glycerine…"

Manning looked at Nina a second, then at the pair of rail-men. "You sons of bitches are batshit crazy."

"Swedish Blastin' Oil," Woodie grinned and softly kissed the clay orb in his hand. "I like to call 'em Bang Balls." He grinned at Nina and made an odd snorting laugh that gave her chills.

"Are we going to let these loons do this?" Manning

looked to the Daggetts still lurking at the threshold of Over There.

Mason shrugged, a Spencer in one hand, a whiskey bottle in the other. "Don't look at me. We're just here for the show."

"Guess I expected as much. Marshal, you going to let them do this?"

"Probably not the best of ideas," Marshal Oden shrugged from the ground; the man still hadn't gotten up. "But I ain't got no others."

Woodie's gap-toothed grin widened. He snickered and peered up at the gap in the ceiling, then went about measuring a couple different angles. Nina wondered how accurate could he be, with those offset eyes seemingly gazing in two slightly different directions.

Everyone stood back as he touched flame to wick, then tossed the bomb up and out of sight. Nina backed away from the door, finding safety near the base of the opposite wall, where the roof seemed strongest. Last thing she wanted was to be caught in another bloody downpour of deadun parts.

A muffled *thud* throttled the air. Dust lifted from the ground and shook loose from the rafters, meeting somewhere in the middle where it choked everyone. A small piece of ceiling fell as Nina covered her mouth with her shirt.

Rachel Buell wailed from the next room as pieces of flesh struck the roof, caught the edges of gaps, or splattered inside the shelter.

"Woohoo!" Woodie spun in a circle.

"That's how you do it, goddamn it!" Strobridge patted

his foreman on the back and clapped.

Manning shook his head. "Another one like that and this place will collapse on top of us. Keep your man reined in."

Strobridge grinned, tipping his hat.

In any case, the pounding and groaning had eerily stopped. Nina put her eye to the knothole, saw nothing, but she wondered what was out there, and how many more would try to get in this night. What evil force was behind it all?

Father Mathias drew a cross on the door with a piece of coal. He placed his hand against the barrier and bowed his head. "God our Father, we thank you for the shelter and comfort of this fort, bless this portal with your strength, O Lord. Help us all through this trying time so to live that we may bring help to others, in the name of the Father, the Son, and the Holy Spirit, one God, forever and ever. Amen."

*T*HEY HAD TO CUT Pa's boot to get it off; now his sausage-swollen foot rested on the rolled up carcass of his footwear. He looked a sorry mess in his tattered shirt, his thick salt-pepper hair and beard just about turned into a right nuthatch's nest.

He groused about it being a mistake letting the rail-boss and his lackey into their group, saying the explosion liked to made him mess his britches.

Nina told him from the way he smelled, wouldn't make much difference. She tried to make him comfortable where he sat against one of the chamber walls. He checked its solidness over and over while Nina applied a wet cloth to his forehead and adjusted the small pile of wood and stone supporting his lower back.

Manning had come in and fussed with her pa's foot, gently moving it into a more comfortable position. "Have to keep it elevated, Lincoln. Helps with the swelling."

"Why are you doing this?" Nina peered at him.

"Doing what?"

Her jaw tightened despite herself. "Being so damn nice to us?"

Manning fixed her with his hard, cobalt eyes. Before he looked away, they softened ever so slightly. "We're in this together. Plain and simple."

"You could have left us behind a half-dozen times. Just an old man and a half-breed." Nina couldn't explain her contempt or the undeniable urge she had to clutch James Manning's jaw and kiss him hard on the lips.

Pa reached out and touched her, a pained grin on his face. "Let's not question Mister Manning's intentions. I, for one, am grateful for what you've done, and I call you a friend. We don't have many."

Nina's face flushed, and she busied herself with fixing a rolled-up cloth behind Pa's neck. "I apologize, Mister Manning. Didn't mean 'nuthin' by it."

"Not necessary. We're all under duress right now, strangers thrown together like...like..."

"...like spiders and scorpions," Pa said.

Manning laughed. "Exactly. And call me James. Now, we got some assholes to deal with, and some...*deaduns*, but we're going to make it."

"Any ideas on what we're really dealing with here?" Pa sounded tired, his voice gruff. It was still uncomfortable cold, and getting colder, too. After settling down a bit, Nina's entire body felt like it had been wrung out. Her neck ached and every muscle in her body felt raw. She couldn't imagine how Pa must feel. It might seem like he'd had an easy trip down to the fort, but hanging on for dear life inside a wheelbarrow weren't no small feat.

"Your guess is as good as mine. I thought it might be the madness, the rabies…"

Nina sat back against the wall next to Pa and looked around. Buck was there, going from window to door to window, spitting tobacco juice and pulling on slabs of wood that had been hammered together from nails scavenged from rafter wood, testing their defenses. Red Thunder stabbed away at the hard earth with his shovel, making two holes for a Dakota fire.

"No," Pa said. "I've seen the madness take dogs and wolves before. It ain't that."

Marshal Oden walked by, tipping his hat to them as he entered the passage to the well. The fact this building had been built over a natural spring was a dern miracle.

"The priest knows what it is," Nina said.

"What do you mean?" asked Pa.

"I mean, he's gotta know something about what's happening here. For one, he doesn't seem all that surprised to see these deaduns. And…" she paused, thinking of how to say it.

"What?" Manning leaned closer, biting into a piece of jerky handed out by Buck earlier. Turned out Red Thunder, Buck, and Father Mathias had brought a decent stock of road supplies, like they'd been traveling together a long time. Nina suspected they might even have a few horses nearby.

"*And*," she said, "he's workin' some kinda magic."

Pa's brow furrowed. "Magic?"

"Yeah." Nina told them about the two times Father Mathias had killed or turned back the deaduns with no more than a touch or a prayer. While she couldn't be positive about the second incident, as she'd not actually seen what happened to the deaduns on the other side of the door, she could certainly attest to the priest's touch. "I think Mister Strobridge knows, too."

Manning nodded. "They did have an interesting conversation earlier. Seems Strobridge chiseled Mathias some time ago, or at least the priest believes so. They were previously acquainted, no doubt, and parted poorly, it seems."

Pa raised his eyebrows and sighed. "Well, I wouldn't have believed in dead folk walking around before today, so a magic-workin' Black Robe sure ain't out of the question." Pa looked back and forth between Nina and Manning. "And to be clear, we agree these are dead folk walkin'?"

Nina nodded.

"Yup," Manning said. "Question is, what do we do about it?"

"Mathias seems amicable enough. He's a man of the Lord. I'm sure if we just asked him..."

"Or," Manning said, "Nina here might privately converse with Red Thunder, bein's they have a shared heritage an' all."

Nina smirked. "The rest of y'all are white. Why don't *you* converse?"

Manning gave Nina a wink. "Problem with that, darlin', is that lying comes too easy to white folks. We speak to Mathias, he's liable to talk us in circles, man of God or not."

Nina snorted. "Worth a shot, I reckon. I'll be back." She got up and ambled to where Red Thunder had just about completed his fire holes. The tribesman was stripped down to just a vest, his sinewy arms were sheened by sweat as he cleared out loose dirt with his shovel.

"Need some help with that?"

The Indian shook his head without even looking up. His nearness frightened Nina, even though they shared something in common. He exuded power. He was a lean, wild man who could kill in a split second. She didn't need a demonstration to know that much.

Nina squatted, thinking about her mother's people, *her* people. What would her mother say to a tribesman? The simpler the better, she thought. Perhaps a plea to join against a common enemy? And who would that enemy be? Living or dead? They didn't have much time in either case.

"I apologize for being so direct, my brother. I've been around white men a long time. Are you *Kuyuidökadö*?"

"*Nimíipuu.*"

"Nez Percé," Nina nodded. "I am Ninataku of the Goshute."

Red Thunder looked up, his gaze lingering a moment. "Shoshone," he said in a slow, gruff voice, naming her people. "But *wasichu*, also."

"My pa…well," Nina stammered. "He's a white man, yes, but a friend to the People." She stuck out her chin. "My ma was named Eluwassee, and she was true Goshute. We lived with them when we could, and we were all welcome, Pa included." Nina's spirit sunk. "My mother was killed by wasichu. Soldiers came in the night…"

"Do you hate them? The *toquashes*?" His voice was low and soft as he spoke the Shoshone word for white soldiers.

Tears threatened to well in Nina's eyes, half because she'd

not expected the question, half because of remembering that damn night. "The ones that killed my ma, yes. But I don't hate all white men. Pa showed me many are kind. Like your priest, I guess."

"*Kind* is probably not the right word for Father Mathias. *Good*, perhaps. But good people are not always kind. Sometimes good people have to make the hardest decisions."

"My pa's that way too." Nina paused and looked askance at the Indian warrior. "You know, brother, I'll listen if you have burdens to share, too. Especially concerning the good father."

Red Thunder put his shovel down, lit some kindling, and tossed it into the hole. He waved his hand over the second hole, driving currents of air in to fuel the flames. "Sister, some burdens are not meant to be shared."

A sense of pride at his acknowledgment of her heritage surprised Nina. She had always been proud, of course, but being called *sister* by Red Thunder seemed like something special. "I have seen Father Mathias do strange things; things I find hard to believe."

"How can you be a sister of mine when you do not believe?"

Nina clamped her teeth, pursing her lips as she picked up a few pieces of ash bark and felt the papery texture. She wasn't sure how to respond.

After a couple seconds, Red Thunder peered at her and asked, "What *do* you believe in, sister?"

"Not the white man's god, that's for damn sure." Nina didn't give a shit if it offended him, it was true.

Red Thunder looked away. He placed some large slivers

of ash bark into the fire, and they ignited quickly under his expert care. "When I first met this strange man in black robes, I believed only in the religion of my people, in the spirits of earth and sky, the eagle, the fox, the bear. But after seeing Mathias work…miracles…" He stared into her eyes again. "It isn't that I believe in his god more than the *weyekin*. It is just that there are many higher things we do not understand, and may never understand, even after we pass into the shadow lands. The higher powers may even be connected; Father Mathias's god to my own guardian spirit. I have come to understand power comes through faith, and Father Mathias has much of that."

Nina found it interesting the warrior spoke so intently about Christianity in light of his own heritage, for the Nez Perce kept their connection to their weyekin, their guardian spirits, very secret and personal. "And you have faith in him? Father Mathias?"

Red Thunder nodded. He took the wispy ash bark from Nina and put it in the fire, watching the flames flare. "I do."

Nina picked up a few pieces of shagbark then, tearing at its roughness with her fingers. "Does he mean us any harm? I mean, me and Pa. And Mister Manning?"

"He has no malice toward those who walk a righteous path. But if you walk with dark spirits, then be warned. You would be wise to listen to him. He understands what is happening here."

"And just what *is* happening here, brother?"

Red Thunder looked at her, and she saw his light brown eyes looked almost golden. "The end of the world," he said.

An ear-shattering wail ripped through the quiet. Nina jerked to her feet. "Rachel."

CHAPTER EIGHT

Chaos ensued in the darkness Over There. Figures pushing and pulling and shoving. More screaming, this time a man. Nina ran into No Man's Land where she was nearly run over by a terrified Jasmine. The black girl careened into Nina, and then tumbled to the dirt.

Nina cast a quick glance her direction. Making sure Jasmine was all right, she looked to find big Marshal Oden and Father Mathias.

Mister Strobridge held a lantern, fiddling with the dial. Once found, he turned it up and bathed the corner in light.

Grover Buell was screaming, arms flailing. A deadun had punched through the wall and was bashing him against it, trying to pull the shopkeeper through the fist-sized hole it had created. The Daggetts struck at the arm with the

stocks of their Spencers, but they might as well have been hitting a piece of lead. The deadun's grip was a vice, its arm a skinless cord of tough, dead meat.

Rachel and Clara wailed for all they were worth, the sounds of their screams sending spikes through Nina's brain.

Grover tried to cover his head with his arm, but to no avail. Nina heard the sickening *crunch* of his skull against the wall, and he screamed no more. For a brief instant, the deadun let go, and then found Grover's wrist, pulling it out through the hole. There was low *snap*, a dry twig *pop*, and Grover exploded to life, his eyes wide with terror and pain. He ripped his bloody arm back through the hole and flopped over on the floor, clutching at it.

Wood and stone blew apart next to Nina's head. A fist punched through and knocked her aside. She pulled her Colt and shoved it into the face of the dead bastard climbing in the window. She blew its brains out, and two more behind it, then she heard the familiar hiss of a burning wick.

One of Woodie's 'Bang Balls' whizzed past her ear, trailing smoke and ricocheting off the top part of the busted window, striking the sill, then bouncing off a deadun's shoulder to fall back into the room. Nina's heart battered her ribs, but there wasn't time to be scared.

She picked up that fucking clay orb of death, expecting it to go off in her hand, and readied to blindly fling it through the window. She stopped herself instead, leapt up, and tossed the sizzler through one of the gaps in the ceiling. She knelt and covered her ears, hoping to hell she'd thrown it hard enough.

A moment later, an explosion cracked the air, a rain of

debris impacting the wall outside, pieces of flesh-bloody shrapnel flying in through the window. Nina spun on Woodie, her gun gripped tight at her side. She wasn't sure what she'd do if she lifted it.

"You cut that fuckin' wick down. I saw it," she accused. He wasn't weaseling his way out of this. "You coulda killed us."

Woodie only smiled that warped grin of his and shrugged.

The sketchy bastard hadn't said two words since they'd met up, but now Nina wanted to smash his face with the butt of her gun. She started in on him but was knocked aside by Manning, who fell on Woodie and pinned him to the ground. The batshit-crazy foreman whimpered as Manning drew back and socked him in the face.

Nina felt a sudden presence behind her. A hand reached under her arm and cupped her breast over her bloody shirt. Another set of fingers slid down the crack of her ass and swept between her legs. Nina yelped and threw an elbow.

"Oof," Strobridge gasped, released Nina, and clutched his stomach. As she turned, he put his fingers to his nose and sniffed them like they were a fancy cigar. His grin was as shit-licking as they came.

Nina raised her Colt, ready to put a bullet into Strobridge's bastard face. Danger was always possible on the trail, but no one had ever gotten close enough to touch her like that. *Ever.*

She glanced at Manning cleaning Woodie's plow but good, the ball-flingin' foreman's face a mess of blood. Maybe between the two of them they could finish these troublemakers once and for all. She wondered who would miss the railroad boss given the circumstances? Easy enough to put the blame on the dead for claiming a couple more.

"Alright, that's enough," Marshal Oden said, pulling James off Woodie after letting him take one more punch. "You made your point."

Woodie lay dazed on the ground, half giggling and half whimpering as he spit out a tooth.

"Hey, ya'll done? We got fucking problems!" George Daggett shouted, firing his Spencer through the wide-open window. Deaduns groaned with urgent hunger, sensing a way in.

Nina didn't give a shit. Let them come. She kept her weapon trained on Strobridge.

"Think on what you're doing, young lady." Father Mathias's voice soothed the chaos. "I'm sure whatever offense Mister Strobridge caused can be amended with an apology. Right, Mister Strobridge?"

"You know me, Father," Strobridge said, grinning. "I admit my own mistakes. I do apologize, ma'am."

Nina cocked her Colt. A hint of doubt flittered in Strobridge's eyes. Just another white man who'd have his way at anyone else's expense, like when they'd come for Ma. And they called *her* people heathens, the goddamned white devils...

"It's still murder," the priest added, gently laying his hand on her shoulder. Strobridge kept staring, sober-faced, as George hollered and popped off another shot.

Nina liked Mathias, and she certainly *wanted* to trust him as much as Red Thunder did, but that didn't mean she had to agree with him. "Ain't no such thing out here... not no more." Nina uncocked her pistol and lowered it. "Why waste the lead? Rather see a deadun get hold of you anyway."

Strobridge's smirk returned. "Now we're back on friendly terms."

Nina shrugged the priest's hand off and turned away. To hell with 'em. If they couldn't hold this side, then they could be vittles for the dead for all she cared. She wasn't saving them from that maniac Woodruff again. Her only concern now was getting Pa and herself out of this bedlam.

She approached their end of the building and stopped cold. In the firelight, the crates stacked in front of the window moved, scooting out from the wall and teetering. Red Thunder had been watching Nina's engagement with Strobridge from the threshold. He caught Nina's expression and turned just as the crates toppled.

Two deaduns crawled through the window and landed in a heap just feet from Pa. The old man fired, shooting one in the shoulder, blowing most its arm off.

Nina rushed forward as Pa crawled away on his belly, the one-armed deadun lurching after him. Red Thunder was there, pushing the corpse down from behind, leaping on its back, and burying his tomahawk in the thing's head.

Meanwhile, Buck slid from the shadows, huge pistol in hand. The remaining deadun—a dapper fellow wearing a gore-stained frocked coat—gave a hungry yawn only to find the barrel of Buck's gun in its mouth. The bullet blew brains and blood to the rafters, putting a fist-sized hole in the wooden shingles above. A four-inch plate of thin, hoary bone spun through the air and landed at Nina's feet.

It was the biggest *wallop* Nina had ever heard, short of Woodie's balls.

Footsteps made her turn. George and Mason Daggett

were on their way over. They must have felt like guardian fucking angels after the bang-up job they'd done saving Grover Buell.

A thought crossed Nina's mind. "Wait! Go back." She waved them away.

George scowled. "Don't tell us what to do, Injun bitch."

"Fine," Nina said, turning to see about Pa. "Stand here like idiots while they slaughter *your* people. Can't you see what they're up to?"

Father Mathias seemed to get it. "Everyone stay your posts! Stay vigilant. I know what this means."

"I'll be," Marshal Oden said, putting his ear to one set of double doors in No Man's Land. "They're coordinating. Drawing us from one side to the other."

Another smash came from Over There, followed by more screaming.

George turned to face the new threat, one hand on his hip. The barrel of his Spencer dragged the ground. "That's just fuckin' great. Deaduns workin' together now? Fuckin' figures."

"Come on," Mason said, pulling George along.

It was a few hours past midnight, nearly half a day since it had all started, and Nina couldn't catch a wink of sleep. Whenever she nodded off, something would slam against one of the wooden barricades or howl at the stars.

Or *Grover*. The poor fellow moaned and caterwauled non-stop on the other side, still delirious from the pounding he'd took.

Nina rolled to her right, peering Over There. She couldn't tell what else was happening, nor did she want to know, but things were at least quiet. She *did* care about the womenfolk, but their fates had been sealed soon as they'd chose *them*.

Mathias and Strobridge sat in two brittle chairs in No Man's Land, probably working out some mysterious bullshit deal, some holdover from the earlier argument. Marshal Oden lay stretched out on the threshold between here and No Man's, tossing and turning with only a rock as a pillow.

The two deaduns who'd fallen through the window Over Here had been shoved out by Buck and Red Thunder, and the crates pushed back in place. Buck had taken some stones from the well wall and put them on top to weigh the crates down. Wouldn't be so easy to push them over next time.

"It's like they're trying to spook us," Pa said from where he and Nina rested against the east-side wall. They'd been forced to move due to the ooze dripping from the rafters where Buck had shot the last deadun. Seemed the safest place next to the well room's entrance. "I tell ya, girl. They're working together to wear us down, waiting till we close our eyes to make some noise. It's going to be a long night. I'm tempted to agree with tossing that idiot Woodruff outside and letting him take a couple hundred of those bastards down with him."

Nina shook her head, too addled to think. Maybe he was right.

"Girl," Pa said. "Help your old man over to the fire. Getting cold."

Manning, Red Thunder, and Buck made room for Nina and Pa as they shuffled over. Pa stretched out on his side, leaning on his elbow, and Nina situated his foot before sitting down. Everyone was reloading and checking their weapons, tossing out ideas about what prospects they had for provisions.

"We got nothing, fellas," Manning said. "Except for what y'all gave us."

"And we thank you for it," Pa added.

Buck shrugged. "Between me and Red, I reckon we got enough vittles to last a few days. Had planned on riding straight through anyway, before we got stuck here." He nodded toward Over There. "Can't say those peckerwoods won't try and take it..."

"They can try." Manning set his jaw.

Nina was curious. "Riding through? Where are your horses?"

"They caught us with our britches round our boots down by some crick. Them *things* got betwixt us and our mounts, herded us up here. Red noticed they move downhill a mite better'n up. Tried circling round, but found this here fort instead. Good thing, reckon, elsewise might o'got our butts surrounded in the flats."

"Too bad. Would be nice to ride the hell out of here."

Manning nodded. "Shit yeah."

"We could eat the bastards," Buck said, spitting juice into the fire.

"What?" Manning pointed outside. "Eat *them?*"

"We got a fire, plenty o' water. I say we drag one in here, chop the biter to bits and cook it." Buck wrinkled his mustache, his coal black eyes filled with mirth, although Nina had no doubt he was deadly serious. "No one would know the difference between that and some o' the slop they serve in these trailside watering holes."

Pa chuckled just before Red Thunder cut in, "Their meat is tainted." His voice was a whisper, yet somehow loud. "If you eat it, the flesh will consume your spirit, and you'll end up just like them."

"Even cooked up good?"

Red Thunder glanced at his friend. "It will consume your spirit."

"Damn. Red's always got rules to things."

"You sayin' you need rules about not eatin' people, Buck?" Nina said. "That's not right."

"I hear tell it's been the going thing around these parts for years. Besides, long as they're seasoned proper..." Buck left off after drawing Red Thunder's stony gaze.

Buck gave a chuckle, "Just tryin' to lighten the mood is all."

They shifted their feet and Manning obliged with a conciliatory snort, but the oppressive fact remained; they wouldn't last very long without food.

Pa laid all the way flat, using his arm as a pillow. His face was red from the warm fire. "One thing's got me worried, boys. I don't think the cavalry is coming. What I mean is, there ain't no militia anywhere near here. And none of our native friends are coming, unless Red Thunder here knows something we don't."

The Indian shook his head and stoked the fire with one of his arrows.

"What do we do then?" Buck toyed with one of the red feathers hanging from his hat.

"Best thing we can do is try to get some sleep," Manning suggested.

"Good luck on that count."

The sounds of groping hands along the walls remained constant, and for a moment, Nina could imagine it driving her crazy if that was all she heard. Then Red Thunder was handing her something around the fire. "What's this?"

"A salve for your father's foot. It will help with the swelling."

Nina took the small wooden box and thanked him. She opened the top and sniffed at the mixture. Herbs and grasses. *Fresh and powerful*, her mother would have called it. "Thank you," she told Red Thunder as she scooted down.

Nina scooped some of the lime green salve out with her finger and held it poised over Pa's swollen ankle. "This might hurt, Pa."

"Go ahead, girl. If it's half as good as what your mother used to concoct, I'll be right as rain in no time."

Nina rubbed the poultice on Pa's tight, shiny skin, careful to avoid pressing too hard. It was true. Her mother had been a powerful healer, curing everything from simple colds to stomach flu, from joint aches to raw wounds. She'd shared much of what she'd known, even though Nina had forgotten most of it. A sudden tear stung her eyes when she realized her mother's medicine kit had burned in the wagon.

"What's wrong, Nina?" Pa sounded sleepy.

"Nothin'. Just thinkin' of Ma."

"She was a wonderful woman. More mysterious than the very sky, I tell ya. I never quite figured her out, and I think she liked it that way."

It was sad to think she had nothing left of her mother's. Nina tried to toughen up. Thinking about dead folks was no good when you had to save your hide, and it didn't bring them back none either, nor do their memories justice. If she and Pa got out of this alive, they'd head straight back to Boa Ogoi and visit Ma's grave. All the graves.

Nina covered his foot completely, the slimy gunk drying into a flaky powder on his skin. "How's that feel?"

Pa snored in reply.

CHAPTER NINE

Something burned Nina's forehead, and her face was wet with sweat. She squeezed her eyes shut and tried to remember where she was. Her ears still rang from all the gunfire. Darkness, death, and blood were all she remembered. All good reasons to let this moment ride on by and fall back into a stupor.

But her face burned.

Nina opened her eyes to find herself staring directly into the sun. She squinted, catching the fragments of a partially collapsed roof and a bare beam once covered by wooden shingles dividing the gap. Nina pulled her hat down and rubbed her eyes, but couldn't get rid of the sting.

Her mouth tasted like she'd et raw shitbird for breakfast. Between the deaduns beating their rotting selves against

their bastion of *faith* and the arguments between the living, there'd been no peace and she'd slept a might fitful and sometimes not at all.

Speaking of fits, an argument seemed to have started up in No Man's Land. She heard Strobridge and Manning's voices raised with smatterings from others. Must have been that and the beam of sun on her face that'd woke her. She yawned and frowned as she rubbed her crusty eyes.

"You awake?" Pa said from right next to her.

"Who can sleep?"

Pa cleared his throat and sighed. "Let's go try'n bridle that ruckus."

Nina whined and sat up, moving out of the sun. "Who cares what they're jawin' about? Me and you just need to figure out what *we're* gonna do."

Pa clicked his tongue. "I hate to say it, but gotta reckon our fates are intertwined like pigs in filth. Ain't nobody movin' without flingin' a little crap our way."

Nina shook her head and sighed, then sat up and ran her tongue around the inside of her mouth. Red Thunder watched them from the other side of the fire. It was impossible to tell if the Indian was tired, pissed off, or about to break into a war dance. In any case, there was an intensity to his every move, a sort of coiled energy.

Nina stretched her neck, moving her head side to side. "That may be true, but you think when the shit flies anyone will check to see if we're keepin' up? They'll leave us high and dry. Every one of 'em."

"Not Mister Manning. He seems a good sort."

"Pa, neither of us know what the man's gonna do. You taught me that."

Pa smiled. Nina could see the pride in his eyes. "I did teach you that."

"We need to make sure we can get to that wheelbarrow when the time comes."

Pa put his hand on Nina's shoulder. "What are you going to do then? Roll me uphill? Push my lard ass down a rock-strewn bank and across Maples Crick? No, girl. Comes to that, you leave me behind and go to high ground."

She glared at him.

"Nina girl, I'll put a bullet in my own head if I got to, and you won't have time to shake that pretty head of yours." Pa took her hand, squeezing hard. "My last, dying wish will always be to give my daughter a chance at life. To be safe and happy. Don't you deny me that, you hear?"

Nina sniffed, knowing he was right, but at the same time not sure she could live without him. She nodded, just to stifle that sort of talk.

"Good. Now let's go see what all the fuss is about. They're making my head throb."

"Stay off the foot, Pa. I'll see what's what." Nina stood on wobbly legs, her whole body sore as hell and her heart stone-heavy. She got some fresh water from the bucket by the well entrance, washed out her mouth, spat, drank down a ladle-full of the brackish stuff. It was cool and had an earthy taste, but felt good going down. Nina re-tied her tangled mess of hair and splashed a little of the cool water on her face. Much better. She needed to piss, but it could wait. She'd hate to miss something important.

Out in No Man's Land, Buck and Manning represented their side, while Strobridge and the Daggetts represented Over There. Marshal Oden and Father Mathias had taken up positions on either side of the group, as if expecting a scrap.

No one was waving any guns around; at least, not yet. That was a start.

She stepped in next to Manning, keeping her hat pulled low over her eyes, just enough to see that son of a bitch Strobridge from the neck down and enough to keep Mean George's Spencer in plain sight.

Manning glanced at Nina. "We're just discussing the possibility of leaving."

"Everyone agrees we can't stay here," Father Mathias nodded, one arm tucked beneath his other arm's elbow and his narrow chin in his hand. "At least not much longer."

"What happened to your bastion of faith, Father?" Nina asked. She didn't mean for it to come out so smart-assed, just wanted to dig a little on the holy man to find out what made him tick. He sure wasn't going to provide information willingly.

Then Mason Daggett decided to add more tinder. "We been waiting for a host of angels and a cavalry of saints and prophets. They not comin'?" He smelled like a damn whiskey still. His brother, George, snickered.

"The bastion of faith is *us*, my daughter. Our spirits. Our *beliefs*. Did you think I meant this ramshackle building, these thin, brittle walls of crumbling adobe and rotten wood?"

"Well, despite whatever's happening here I still don't believe in your god, Father, and I'm guessin' these hilljack Daggetts don't, either. That probably messes up your plans, huh?"

"No, my daughter." She sensed Mathias's smile even

though her eyes were down. "It only strengthens my resolve to bring you all into the light."

"Question ain't if we're leavin'," Mason Daggett said, sneering, "it's when. As in, right fuckin' now. That's this hilljack's vote." Mason tossed a little volume at Nina.

"Mine too," his brother chimed in, then added "Injun bitch" under his breath.

"You'd best stow that talk," Manning said low to Mean George.

"Or what?"

Nina turned slightly. "Hey, I don't need you speaking up for me," she said sidelong.

"Excuse me, but it ain't just for you. I'm tired of this blowhard's gas."

George's screw-mouth twisted up and his eyes tightened, but it was Mason who spoke up, stepping forward face-to-face with Manning. "Fuck you, ya Yankee bastard."

"I'm no Yankee," Manning said, pushing his face closer until the brim of his hat touched Mason's forehead. "And you need to lay off the rot-gut."

"Sock him in the beezer, Mase." George gripped his rifle and licked his lips. "I'm right behind ya."

"Why don't you shut your hole," Nina said through clenched teeth, touching her palm to the Colt Navy on her hip.

"Settle down, goddammit!" Marshal Oden growled, wedging in between Manning and Mason and separating them with his square-shouldered girth. "We need to come together, now. Christ have mercy. Deaduns at the door and here you are ready to skin on one another."

There was a tense moment as everyone glowered, all

except for Buck Patterson who Nina noticed had walked up with a bemused expression. Manning broke the silence. "You're right, Marshal." He took a step back. "We all seem a bit frayed at the ends."

"With good reason," said Oden, turning to make sure Mason and George were backing down, as well. He looked at Nina, then at her hand on the grip of her gun. "But the last thing we need is to go heels on one another. Now, what about the rest of them?"

Manning gestured to the Other Side and then back toward Pa. "You gonna leave the women behind? How about the hobbled man in the next room?"

Nina peered past Manning's shoulder, past the priest, and saw Jasmine standing with her arms crossed, watching everyone. The woman looked tired and in low spirits. No surprise there. Nina nodded to her, and Jasmine returned the smallest hint of a nod.

"We never said nothin' about leaving nobody behind," Mason said.

"But we can't drag em along with us—"

"Goddammit, George." Mason sounded exasperated with his brother. Not because George was a complete asshole, but that he was potentially tipping their hand—least that's how Nina saw it.

"We don't know how many of them things are out there," said Marshal Oden, removing his hat and rubbing the top of his balding head. "Could be a hundred, could be a thousand."

"What are the deaduns doin'?" Nina thought it was a fair question.

"Look through any of these holes and all you'll see is

them standing there doing nothing." That was Strobridge.

"Yeah, they ain't doin' *shit*," George affirmed.

"Mayhap someone needs to climb topside and have a look around," Buck offered.

"Needs to be someone small enough not to bring the roof down on our heads," Mason added, then belched under his breath as he eyeballed Nina.

"Listen, everyone," Father Mathias spoke, raising his hands for quiet. They looked to the priest, but he just stood there, hands up, kind of looking everywhere and nowhere all at once.

Then, Nina noticed it, too. Total silence. Not a single moan or spine-shuddering cry from outside. Only Grover Buell's quivering complaints reached them from his makeshift pallet Over There. Nina thought about what Red Thunder had said, about the deaduns being tainted, and she wondered to what end Grover's feverish path might lead.

Nina turned to Mathias, lifting her gaze. In the morning light, the priest's eyes were as crystal blue as the surface of a lake. She noticed his trimmed beard and mustache. Properly representing the Lord, she supposed. "I'll go up top, but I'll need someone to boost me." She glared at Strobridge. "Not you."

The man smirked and tipped his Stetson.

They looked around for a good spot to put her, finding a place where two beams crossed above the doors they'd come through last night. There was a small place where the wooden slats looked rotted and weak, a hint of light passing through.

Manning put one hand on her shoulder, pointed up with the other. "Now, see where the beams go? Try to stay on them, near the edges if you can. You'll have more support there."

Nina had already figured that out, but she nodded anyway, tossing her hat down.

Manning and Buck cupped their hands and squatted. Nina put one boot into James's waiting hands and then, with her fingers stretched on their backs for support, stepped up into Buck's.

She gasped as they threw her faster than she expected. Her arms instinctively shot up to cover her head. Her fists met resistance, but then she grasped for purchase through what was left of the old, rotted wood.

Having gotten Nina's feet to their chests, the fellas adjusted their grips and pushed her higher. Nina leaned forward, using her legs now, scrambling and straining until she lay face down on the roof, spitting out bits of moss-covered wood.

She got to her knees, gagging on the stench of rotted meat, which hung thick in the morning air. Her stomach churned, threatening to eject the swallow of water she'd had for breakfast. And then it did, the acrid liquid spewing past her lips to splash on the roof.

Nina squeezed her eyes shut and growled away the pain.

"You okay up there?"

"Yeah," Nina waited for her roiling stomach to settle and opened her eyes. She wiped away a line of drool hanging from her mouth and looked up...

...impossible...

...several hundred, maybe a thousand, deaduns filled her field of vision. They stood around the bedraggled blockade's interior like herded cattle, staring straight ahead with blanched, lifeless eyes. Motionless but for some silent jawing, stretching their mandibles and exposing their broken, jagged teeth, an impregnable wall of flesh and bone nearly as far as she could see.

The affliction did not discriminate between race, color, or creed. A family stood holding hands in a grisly display of affection. The little girl's bonnet sat cockeyed on her head, splashed with dark brown stains. A contingent of rail workers still held picks and axes, dressed in grungy frocks and wide-brimmed hats that cast shadows over their yellow faces. Their boss stood swaying at the front, one arm hewn above the elbow, his remaining fist clenched at his side.

In the daylight, more details burned themselves into Nina's brain. Some deaduns seemed risen straight from the grave, barely held together by sinew. Maggots and beetles burrowed thick inside torsos, causing their skin to undulate like waves on water. Others were newer; fresh bloat, swollen insides bursting at the seams, bits oozing through the blackened cracks. Nina had a thought and gagged again; what would all this rotted flesh have smelled like in the heights of summer?

And what was this? On the deaduns' exposed skin were faint symbols like foreign writing traced in weaving lines around forearms, faces, and chests. Had she noticed this before? Likely impossible in the panic and fading light of last night, but what did it mean? She decided right then that this was no malady, no sickness gone wild.

Her first instinct was to run, or just fall back down into the hole and forget she'd even come up here, but she had a job to do. Besides, there was *nowhere* to run. Nina stepped around the perimeter of the building, testing each wooden shingle with the front of her boot before applying her weight. The roof inclined slightly to the west, tilting down to direct runoff. Nina followed the edge, stopping to look around every few feet. They were completely surrounded by deaduns.

She made out the wall around the fort, sharpened logs piercing upward into a fog rolling in from the hills, very similar to the haze that had followed the undead last night. Dark clouds clustered overhead, moving by too quickly, the sun disappearing and reappearing as patches went by.

Nina felt another swell of hot panic, but she put a lid on it before it boiled over. Her eyes probed the multitudes as she maneuvered to the front, trying to see a way through. The stench had become almost bearable, but there was no way in Hell she'd ever get used to it. She didn't *want* to get used to it…

Nina's gaze stopped on a peculiar figure amidst the stinking, swaying corpses. He stood stiffly, donned in white robes with long, wide-mouthed sleeves. His hands were locked together before him, head covered by a faded yellow cowl. He seemed regal, somehow. Old.

He weren't no deadun. This feller was a living, breathing person standing devil-may-care in the very midst of all that undead flesh.

So why did they not attack him? Was this possibly the one behind this moving mass of decomposing flesh? Of a sudden, she was derned sure of it, though she couldn't say how.

Only one way to find out.

Nina drew her Colt and took aim, putting the tip of her sight in the center of the man's hood. She cocked the hammer, pulled the trigger...and a deadun intercepted her bullet. It stepped in front of Yellow Hood at the last second, and the left side of its head exploded. It flopped to the ground. Yellow Hood remained in place, though he turned toward her.

"What's going on?" Manning hollered up. "You okay?"

She took aim again, but before she could fire, more deaduns stepped in the way, blocking the figure from view. Bastard had himself a meat shield. She eased the hammer home and retracted her weapon.

"Shit." Nina was shocked at the deliberate ploy. These things couldn't take orders, could they? But she knew better. She'd seen it back in Coburn Station. Deaduns doing the bidding of someone else, but for what purpose? It was frightening, and also confusing. Nina and Pa, and the rest of their little party, were just regular folks. Fucked up, maybe, but still relatively regular by all standard conventions. What would anyone like Yellow Hood want with them?

"I'm coming down," she called out.

Nina made her way around the perimeter in the eerie presence of a thousand silent deaduns. She could feel their milky eyes on her, hungering to pull her down and strip her flesh away. She thought about taking a shortcut, crossing down the middle, but couldn't be sure she wouldn't bring the whole roof down. After what seemed like forever, she made it to the hole and peered down. Manning and Buck looked up, ready to receive her.

Nina slid down in a hurry, so fast she didn't see the sliver of wood until it was too late. The sharp piece scraped her side as the fellas gathered her in. "Shit," she said, checking the wound to find it was only a scratch. Painful, but harmless.

Rachel and Clara Buell suddenly cried out, their high-pitched screams ripping everyone's attention Over There. The women were backing away from where Grover sat against the far wall. The shopkeep had seemed nearly dead just a second ago and had probably startled them with his abrupt rise.

But that wasn't all. Twin orbs of black stared back at them from where his eyes used to be. Round, bottomless marbles that made Nina think of a bug or a lizard. They were the same eyes that had stared back at her from the faces of those deaduns last night. The same as the ones outside that gathered to shield Yellow Hood.

Jasmine, standing nearby, gasped and dropped a bucket of water.

"Pappy!" Rachel screamed, her mother struggling to keep her from running to her father. Marshal Oden strode to help, grabbing the girl by the arm. "Let me go," she yanked to no avail.

"Stop it," the marshal told her, also to no avail as the girl kept yanking.

From the face of Grover Buell came a long, pointed tongue. It slithered across his lips and cheeks, licking the chapped face before retreating. The thing inside Grover poured its oily gaze over them, its eyes sending a chill up Nina's spine. "Let the girl come to her father," it said with a mock smile.

Gun barrels raised and pointed. The clicks of cocking weapons cut the air.

"Guns, guns, guns," it said, still smiling. "And those *wonderful* balls of Mister Woodruff's. I'll be happy when you lay your bag of explosives at my feet after you've been turned." Its accent was the same cut-down English those Celestial coolies used, only more graceful, filled with menace as the words spilled from Grover's lips.

Woodie, his face a swollen mess from Manning's beat-down, chuckled uncertainly from his corner of the room.

"Grover, why are you doing this?" Clara Buell asked.

Marshal Oden shoved both women toward Buck Patterson. "Get them out of here."

The roughrider nodded and manhandled the women out while Clara kept asking, "What…what has happened to Grover? Why is this happening?"

Buck didn't answer, just drew them away with Jasmine's help, the black woman putting her hands on Rachel's shoulders as the young girl wept and wailed.

The blood curdled in Nina's veins and she shifted from foot to foot, found herself moving closer to James Manning as Grover's black orbs settled on Father Mathias. "Hello again, Thomas. You have something I want."

Blamed if everyone wasn't letting on with their acquaintance to this mysterious Black Robe. Nina wasn't sure what to think of that, but her mistrust of the man just went up a few more notches.

Father Mathias inclined his head. "Liao. I wondered how long it would take you to find me."

Grover's face went slack, his brow relaxing above those hideous orbs. "I followed the stench of false hope, the sound of doomed prayers, the bleating of blind sheep."

Father Mathias, keeping a respectable distance from the possessed shopkeep, crossed his arms and smiled. "No need to be nasty, Liao."

Grover's face became hard again, the scrapes he'd

accumulated on his head and face oozing puss from some internal pressure. "I want what is rightfully mine."

"But it isn't *yours*—"

"Give me the Taiping Jing or you will die horribly, Thomas! Alone. Screaming for your whore of a mother, renouncing your charlatan faith! A turning will be the best you'll get. I'll play with your soul for a century, torturing you until torture becomes all you know, all you remember of your pathetic life."

"That's good, Liao. More ferocious than last time. You've been working on your delivery."

"Thank you, Thomas," the Grover-thing snickered. "I've had time to practice, but it doesn't make my threat any less real." Its eyes roamed across Nina and the rest of the group, and a fawning smile formed. "If you hand him over to me, I'll go. You will wake up to find me and my *heavenly* subjects removed."

"You can't make a pact with a devil," Mathias said. "He'll kill us all, regardless of your cooperation. Besides, he's been planning this for a long time. Even if you survived, the world as you know it would be gone in a year or two."

"I would have been content to wait, savoring my sure victory, but you summoned me by thieving the Taiping Jing."

"It doesn't matter, Liao. I don't have it." Mathias gestured at the railroad boss, whose eyes widened. "Mister Strobridge here stole it from me. It's him you want."

Nina was pleased to see the bastard's terrified look. He backed up two or three steps before bumping into a stone-faced Red Thunder. The Indian nudged Strobridge forward.

"Is this true, railroad man? You have what I seek?" The refined tone sounded strange coming from Grover's mouth, bloody spittle accentuating each word with a gurgle.

"No, I...I don't...well, not exactly," Strobridge stammered, coming forward and holding his hands out. "I don't have it with me..."

Grover's face twisted, the split brows lowering.

"But I can get it," Strobridge quickly added.

"I give you until tomorrow morning to turn both of these men over to me, or my heavenly subjects will cleanse this place. Don't think of doing anything foolish, or else I will have no mercy. Consider tonight a gift. Revel in it, but know it comes to a quick close."

Suddenly, Mason Daggett stepped forward and opened up with his Spencer. Nina jumped at the sound, but was even more shocked to see Grover still smiling from where he sat, two fingers held up together, no evidence of a bullet wound to be seen.

The rest of them fired, blasting Grover with a wall of leaden death. Bullets should have torn him to pieces, yet they didn't leave a mark. Grover pulled an even bigger grin, hair whipping around his head with the turbulence of the lead balls. A pattern of chipped stone and rock dust began to form around the shopkeep and the room filled with gunsmoke.

Rachel and Clara rushed back in, Jasmine and Buck behind them. The Buell women screamed and clung to one another as bullets plowed the rock around their father and husband.

Nina's aim was true, but she still missed, her bullets shrugged aside by some invisible shield. Maybe this was some kind of devil. She ran out of slugs and lowered her weapon, shaking her head.

The Daggetts were still firing, and it appeared the thing in Grover was weakening. The grin left its face. Its hand shook. A bullet buried itself in Grover's chest. Another obliterated the shoulder holding up the fingers.

The entity vacated Grover Buell; Nina didn't understand how she knew, only that those black eyes were replaced with Grover's sad, expressive ones. Before anyone realized he was a living man again, their bullets pierced his already broken body, slamming him into the stone. The shopkeep bucked and twisted as projectiles laid waste to him, until one of Buck's massive slugs slammed into his cranium and blew poor Grover's head all over the wall.

CHAPTER TEN

DISTANT CHANTS REACHED NINA in her black dream. Drums pounded *bom-bom-ta-ta, bom-bom-ta-ta,* forming a strong trunk of sound. The step-skip cadence of Gaiute feet moved against the earth, smooth as branches waving in the wind. Voices, like stirring leaves, sang to her, comforting her spirit and filling her with peace and tranquility. The steps and voices combined to form one mighty tree, one ancient song—the song of her Shoshone brothers and sisters.

Yet even in this tranquil place, hands of bone reached for her in the darkness. Rotted teeth, jagged and sharper in death, snapped all around. They wanted to consume not only her body, but her soul. Nina choked on the suffocating stench of the undead. She didn't care about her body. Let

them have it. But the thought of her spirit dying without release terrified her.

Nina's spiritual brothers and sisters responded, lifting her up from the darkness with their song. She couldn't understand why at first. She barely knew them. After the soldiers attacked her tribe when she was a girl, she and Pa spent only small periods of time among the Bannock tribes and among those the white man called Snake People, Locust Eaters, and the Wind River People, and this was only when Pa allowed some reprieve from the trail. It had hardly been enough for them to ever be considered part of any tribe.

Blood is blood, my daughter, the Shoshone said, as one.

Strength surged through her, crushing all fear and desperation. Her heart beat strong and fierce. An eagle's call swept through the ranks of undead, scattering them into ash. Nina's spirit wept with joy, and she opened her eyes.

Copper-skinned people with long, serious faces stared down at her. Their high-cheeks glowed in firelight, shuffling, moccasin-covered feet kicking up dust. Covered in deer skins adorned with beads of aqua, jade, and blood red, they encircled her, pouring their love over her like summer-warmed honey. One with the land; one with Nina.

She caught the scents of cooking meat, and her stomach became full. She felt fresh, cool water in her throat, and she was no longer thirsty. The drums beat the weariness from her body, and she was alive.

Her gaze fell to a tribesman sitting cross-legged before her, suddenly there, or perhaps he had always been. Wrinkles lined his face, and deep frown lines etched the corners of his mouth. Two braids of hair—one over each shoulder—hung gray with age. An immense eagle-feathered headdress rested on his brow. He regarded Nina with brown eyes as deep and wise as time itself.

She recognized him as the *boha gande*, the tribal shaman, and bowed her head in an instinctive gesture of respect.

"Ninataku, Fire-Eater, raise your head." His voice shook the ground beneath her, for he *was* the very earth. "You have faced many dangers, but you have overcome them. Your spirit is strong."

Nina sat taller, a smile touching her face. "Thank you, boha gande."

"You have proven yourself worthy of our greatest blessing, so we bestow upon you the strength of our people to help you see things through to the end."

"The end?"

"Yes, there is much more for you to do. Very little time."

"I don't know *what* to do, Pa is hurt, and we're trapped…"

"Neither you nor your father's physical bodies are important. You must save the land, for without it, all life will die. Right now, a great poison runs through it, an infection that must be purged."

"But *how?*"

The boha gande's eyes turned to the night sky, his ears listening to some message Nina could not hear. "Ninataku, I'm here to tell you your mother's spirit travels with you. She loves you and will guide you on your journey. There will be many perils along the way, many things to test your heart. Now, you must go…"

Desperation shook Nina, panic like a cold spike sunk into her spine. She would have to leave this place, leave the protective arms of the People, and go back to something…

horrible. It wasn't fair to show her such peace, and then throw her back to the world of the living dead. "I don't want to go. Allow me to stay, boha gande. I'll learn what I must, I'll—"

"We are but spirits in your dreams, shadows from the world beyond. You are still flesh, Ninataku. We are but dust and memory."

Sadness overwhelmed her. She wanted to shout out, to raise her fists and demand a place with her people. And where was her mother? Surely, she was here. Nina could stay with her.

But what about Pa? Who would look after him?

"Goddamn it." The words slipped out before she could stop them.

The boha gande only smiled. "Now go, Fire-Eater, with the blessing of the tribe."

Crystal teardrops fell from her lashes. She opened her mouth to speak, but a crack of lightning shattered the sky.

Nina opened her eyes with a gasp.

Manning smiled at her from where he sat against the wall. "Sleep talker."

No, *Fire-Eater*. It took Nina several seconds to orient herself. She longed to go back to sleep, but the oppressiveness of knowing the deaduns were out there and the reeking stench of blood on her clothing piqued her brain. The beautiful song in her head faded into a dull hum, then disappeared.

She yawned, her ears popped. "What did I say?"

"Sounded like you were singing actually."

Her eyes looked through the gap in the ceiling at the night sky. Stars hung there like gods watching this bloody nightmare play out for the second night. Nina hoped they were amused.

She gazed around the room, realizing for the first time the absence of that deep chill in her bones. Red Thunder's fire radiated, emitting very little smoke; not that it mattered at this point. Buck squatted with his back to the flames, a bottle of whiskey hanging from his hand. Father Mathias, Mister Strobridge, and Marshal Oden sat in chairs in No Man's Land, talking low; probably some narrative about what to do about their ghastly visitor from earlier, and who'd give up the Taiping Jing or whatever the hell it was.

Red Thunder stared at her from across the fire. His eyes glowed in the firelight, lending to his already intense gaze. They were from two different worlds, but their connection was clear. Did he know about her dream? Had he also dreamt about *his* tribe?

Jasmine, Rachel, and Clara had come across to this side, unable to stand being in the same room with Grover's blood and brains decorating the wall. The smell lingered despite all they'd done to clear the air. They were a snuggling huddle of hair and arms in the southwest corner. Not the most ideal place to be, between a door and a window, but at least they'd fallen asleep. And Buck watched over them, even if their visitor—Liao of the Yellow Hood—had said there would be no more trouble until tomorrow. That's just what a villain might say before attacking. Damned if any of them should relax their guard just because some deadun-bating maniac obliged to lay off a spell.

Nina turned her head to the left and surveyed her pa snoring lightly, a colorful, woven blanket pulled up to his chin. One of Red Thunder's. She reached over and stretched it to cover his shoulder. "He been sleepin' okay?"

Manning yawned. "For a few hours. Deaduns ain't been back. Guess you would have known if they had. Been quiet Over There, too. Maybe they done settled down at last. I tell ya, those Daggetts and..."

Nina shook her head. She didn't want to think about Mister Strobridge, creepy Woodie, or the Daggetts. She didn't believe for one second they'd settled down, but she was filthy, covered with blood and muck, and all she wanted to do was wash it off.

Nina stood. Her joints should have been aching, her muscles sore and strained. But they weren't. Even her neck had lost its stiffness. She looked at Manning and the exhaustion was plain to see on him, his eyes a bit sunken and a hint of dark stubble lined his firm, angular jaw. He put his head back against the wall and Nina watched his Adam's apple bob as he swallowed. She needed a drink.

The sound of drums still echoed in her ears as she made her way over to Buck. "Scaly bastards gave up some bug juice, did they?"

Buck's face turned up, but his eyes remained shadowed. "Traded three buckets of water for it." He held the bottle up.

"That's a good trade." Nina took the bottle and inhaled from its mouth. The whiskey fumes cleared the rank smell from her head. She turned the sloshing liquid up, taking three healthy swigs. It burned like a sonofabitch going down, her face screwing up all sour, but her stomach welcomed the jolt. Her head swam pleasantly. She took another swig for good measure before handing the bottle back with a word of thanks.

Buck nodded and drank.

Nina ducked into the well passage, running her hands along the walls as she went, guided by the meager campfire light. It was cold and damp, solid. Even the ceiling was stone. The well room was half the size of the others, filled with old crates stacked to the ceiling, rusted lanterns, and other supplies that had gone bad. One crate had been broken up, the pieces now drying next to Red Thunder's fire. If the stuff burned properly, they'd be warm for a few days. Hungry, but warm. If they lived that long.

In the near pitch black, Nina made out a short stone wall in the corner marking the well opening, and she went and sat down. Peering down into the dark depths, she was greeted with a cold breeze across her cheeks. She dropped the bucket and turned the crank counter-clockwise to lower it. Soon, she had a sloshing pail of cool water resting on the well wall.

Nina put her hat down and tied her hair out of her face. She dipped the rag into the bucket and patted at her neck, scrubbed her face vigorously, gasping every time the cold touched her. She wrung out the rag and held it up. Frowned. Her eyes had adjusted to the dim light and she could see it was dark with mud, blood, and whatever else.

Goosebumps raised on her shoulders and chest as she unbuttoned her shirt and wiped down her breasts. Her arms were the worst, covered with grime she could hardly stand to look at, fingernails stained red around the edges, scrapes and bruises she couldn't see but knew were there. She pulled off her boots and socks and rolled up her pants legs, running the rag over her feet until they were relatively clean. Soon, the rag was completely ruined, and she couldn't wash it out no matter how hard she tried.

"Need another?" Nina started and looked up. Jasmine stood there holding an old leather bag and a short candle. She'd found an old coat, too.

"I took the bag out of that wagon before we left. Stuffed it full of things. I'm pretty sure there's a rag or two in here."

"I'm almost done…" Nina stopped herself before she could push the girl away. She had no right to feel betrayed. Jasmine had good reason to go with the Daggetts when they'd arrived here, had probably saved them all some grief. Jasmine wasn't hers to tell what to do.

Nina relaxed. "You know, I reckon I could use another. I'm covered."

"I know." Jasmine set her candle down and opened the bag's latch, fishing inside. She handed an old cotton shirt to Nina. "You look a lot better though. Can hardly tell you've been standing knee deep in guts."

Nina chuckled, drying herself off. "Knee deep in guts. That's about right. I might be a little cleaner, but my clothes are done for."

Jasmine's face brightened. "Hey, I've got some clothes. Some denims and a shirt. Too small for me, but oughta fit you just fine. Nancy had grabbed 'em for herself but… you're more than welcome to them."

"Thanks." Nina paused, not sure how to ask her next question. "Did they—?"

Jasmine looked confused for a moment, but her look softened. "Naw, they didn't do nuthin'," Jasmine laughed, her voice rich and smooth, heavy with exhaustion. "Georgie couldn't get his little pecker hard with the Buells standin' around and a preacher in the next room. Worst part was listening to them complain about having to trade away their whiskey. Talked a little about taking the well away from y'all, but they're all bark and no bite. Anyway, I'm free now."

Nina shot her a quick smile. "I shouldn't have worried. Seems you can take care of yourself just fine."

"I can, but it's nice when someone else takes care of me, too. Mind if I sit?"

"Go right ahead."

Nina thought she'd just meant to sit down on the crate, or at the very least *nearby*. But Jasmine plopped down on the well wall right next to her, stiflingly close, her dress covering Nina's bare foot, one leg tucked beneath her and the other on the floor.

"Let me see." Jasmine reached over before Nina could protest. The black woman ran her fingers through Nina's hair, trailing down, down, past her shoulders, until the strands feathered away between her fingertips. Jasmine's hand brushed Nina's arm before pulling away, sending a chill down her back.

"You got long, pretty hair...except for that missing clump." Jasmine smiled, repeating the motion, toying with the frayed ends Nina had sawed off fighting the deadun.

This time Nina closed her eyes and leaned into the touch. A light gasp escaped her lips, a tiny hitch of breath. Why was her belly full of butterflies? She opened her eyes. "Can you make it look better?"

Jasmine frowned and drew back, her hands falling on Nina's shoulders. "With what?"

Nina pulled out her hunting knife and wiped it clean with the rag. She turned it over and handed it, hilt-first, to Jasmine.

Jasmine glanced down. "Hope you ain't expecting

anything special. Gonna be ugly if we use that."

"Just cut it short. Ain't gotta be perfect."

Jasmine shrugged, taking the hilt and testing its weight. "You asked for it. Just don't come after me once you look in the mirror."

Nina bent her head forward, and Jasmine leaned in, loosing Nina's hair. The woman went to work, pulling long sections and shredding them away, tossing the remnants on the floor. Nina was sad to see it go, but she had no particular love for her hair, anyhow. Got in the way more often than not. With the deaduns likely to tear it out, she figured it made sense to cut it short.

Jasmine's soft touches left Nina feeling strange but comforted, her brain buzzing from the attention. She shut her eyes and sunk further, her forehead coming to rest on Jasmine's soft chest as the woman made sense of the back.

"Knife's sharp. Maybe it won't be so bad."

Nina breathed deep. By this time, only faint traces of Jasmine's flowery perfume remained. All that was left was her strong, natural odor and leftover mingled scents of blood and grime. Weren't none of them too pretty at the moment, but somehow Jasmine shone through the mess. The way she held herself. The way she moved. The way she touched. Nina couldn't imagine what the woman must look like dressed to the nine's.

Jasmine set the knife down and leaned back, tousling Nina's hair with both hands. She laughed. "Not too bad."

Nina reached up and pushed Jasmine's coat back, put her hands on the woman's shoulders, feeling their solid form beneath her fingers, marveling at her light copper skin against Jasmine's dark. Nina lowered her gaze, running her hands down the woman's lean arms, tucking them beneath Jasmine's elbows, and wrapping her in an embrace. Nina smiled when Jasmine shrugged off her coat and returned the squeeze. They pressed themselves together in unabashed affection, strangers just hours ago, worlds apart, now finding solace in one another.

As much as she loved Pa, he'd only taught her fear and mistrust of others. Rightfully so perhaps, but Pa's occasional bear hugs couldn't take the place of a friend's embrace, a *woman's* embrace. Like when she'd worked with her mother in the garden so long ago. Simple days with simple chores, her mother's soft hands on Nina's face, that reassuring feeling that Nina was loved—this was similar, but not *exactly* the same. Pleasant, either way.

The revelation left her feeling sad for her pa, sad for *herself*, and she missed Ma more than ever. Tears ran down Nina's face and wet Jasmine's shoulders.

Jasmine clenched harder. "Oh, Nina. You poor thing."

"Nuthin' poor about me," Nina said, her lips pressed against Jasmine's shoulder. "Just tired and worried, I guess."

"And here I thought I was the frightened one."

Nina laughed, her lips salty with her own tears and Jasmine's sweat. "I'm scared shitless," she whispered.

"Well, there's two of us, then."

A piece of broken crate crunched. A shadow moved over them. Nina jerked away, reaching for her knife.

"Easy, honey." The figure's hands went up in a defensive gesture. "It's just me."

Nina showed Strobridge the point of her knife, unsure if she was mad about the interruption, or if she simply didn't like the man, then realized it was both. "Might want to announce yourself next time, asshole."

"Hey, I'm visitin' fair and square. Traded another bottle of whiskey for more water. Your people drive a hard bargain." Strobridge's eyes roamed over Jasmine's body and switched to Nina, lingering on her open shirt. Nina wiped her wet eyes and resisted the urge to cover herself, unwilling to let the railroad boss know he made her uncomfortable.

Strobridge pressed his lips together, his eyes losing their relaxed joviality. "And while we're on the subject of bargains." He reached into his coat, pulling out a clip full of money. The boss counted out two bills and dropped them between the two women. "A hundred a piece if I can get both your asses up here side by side for a double screwing."

Nina ground her teeth, a flush rising in her face. "Fuck you."

"Aw, now. No need to be upset about it. Take it or leave it."

"Leave it. C'mon." Nina offered her hand to Jasmine.

Jasmine gave Nina an apologetic look and picked up both bills, stuffing them into a pocket. "It's a lot of money." She stood and began spreading her coat over the stone wall.

Strobridge snickered. "You sure you don't want in on this, Injun girl? I love me some squaw."

Nina fumbled for something smart to say; a stinging insult would have been nice. "I like real men, you son of a bitch," was all she could think of.

"Didn't look like that a second ago. Must be true about your folk being free spirits, touching each other's Injun titties..."

Nina's hand went to her hip, but her gun was out there with Manning and Pa. And before Nina could get herself into real trouble with the railroad boss, Jasmine turned and held out a clump. "Here's them clothes I promised." Her eyes held a thousand apologies, but she wasn't afraid. And again, Nina felt like an idiot for thinking Jasmine didn't have to make her own way in this world. But what was so damn wrong about caring for someone?

Nina snatched the denims and shirt out of Jasmine's hand, moved a pace or two away and turned to the side. If she stormed out now, Strobridge would have won, and she couldn't very well get changed out there in front of all those other men. She wasn't worried about Pa and Manning, but had no idea about Buck or anyone else out there, though she was beyond angry at them for letting Strobridge back here in the first-fucking-place. At least it was dark in the well room.

She moved the bucket to the side and unbuttoned her blood-crusted shirt while Jasmine pulled up her dress and bent over. Nina caught a glimpse of Jasmine's long dark legs and bare backside before averting her gaze. Strobridge unbuckled his belt and dropped his pants. There was a rustle of clothing and a gasp from Jasmine.

Nina glanced up and caught the railroad boss's bearded face pointed her way while he worked his *thing* into Jasmine. Nina hated being part of the display, but she wasn't about to let Strobridge shake her. He kept his head turned her way in the dark as he moved his hips harder and harder, grunting as he worked. Jasmine let out soft gasps to the rhythm of Strobridge's thrusts.

Nina used the rag real quick to wipe the blood caked in her waist area, getting out dried up scabs and other things she couldn't quite describe. She worked her shirt and overalls off, biting her lip as she got naked, then quickly pulled on the clean shirt and trousers hoping Strobridge hadn't been able to see anything in the dim light.

Petty feelings of betrayal gnawed at her. What did it matter who Jasmine fucked? Why was Nina sore about her making two-hundred damn dollars? It wasn't that. What bothered her was that arrogant shit-stain who thought he owned everyone, waltzing in here and interrupting a much-needed quiet moment, trying to make the women feel embarrassed and flashing his paper *and* his pecker.

Nina pulled on her boots, tucked her pants in them, and snatched up her hat. By this time, Strobridge had worked himself into a frenzy, hands gripping Jasmine's hips, thighs slapping against her ass. Nina glared at his stupid, lustful grin—good thing she didn't have her six-gun right now because she'd shoot that demonic grin off the bastard's goddamn face.

Instead, she picked up the sopping, bloody rag, and tossed it at him. She'd only meant to get him a little wet, but her throw went high. The rag splattered against his face and rolled down between him and Jasmine and landed hanging from his cock.

"In case you need to clean up after," she said.

"Goddamn it!" Strobridge sputtered as Nina strutted out of the well room with a scowl on her face.

CHAPTER ELEVEN

Nina figured Strobridge would be jacked up from the humiliation and come tearing out with his pants half down, ready to break her neck. She hoped he tried, too. Give her an excuse to shoot the sonofabitch dead, increasing her and Pa's chances of getting out of here alive. No doubt he had enough money to buy off the Daggetts, which would make it hard for them to turn him over to that Liao character. Hell, he could probably buy everyone here except for Father Mathias; maybe Manning, too.

The way Nina saw it, if someone didn't tip the scale right now, there'd be a reckoning soon...and it wouldn't be between the living and the dead.

She waited for Mister Strobridge to come out, only he didn't, not right away. So, she sidled up next to the fire,

tossing in tiny sticks, watching Pa sleep while Manning, Red Thunder, and Buck conversed quietly nearby. She narrowed her eyes at them as she strapped her gun belt about her waist. She'd be giving Manning a talking-to at the very least.

Much to her dismay, the railroad boss exited the well chamber with a grin on his face, holding a full bucket of water. Other than a red stain around his collar and tie, he looked right as rain. Even gave Nina a wink as he went by.

Nothing at all right about that.

Nina eyed the passage, waiting for Jasmine to come out. After a minute or two, Nina got worried and thought she might have to go in and fetch her. A dark feeling descended on her. Maybe she'd underestimated the railroad boss. Maybe he'd killed Jasmine, stabbed her, or pushed her down the well…

Nina sighed when the woman finally *did* come out, walking on wobbly legs, a whiskey bottle dangling from her hand. Jasmine sat down heavily, awkwardly, crossing her legs and lifting the bottle to her lips. A swath of her curlicue hair fell back, drawing an angry glare from Nina, a spark of red hot anger igniting behind her eyes. Jasmine had been hit. *Hard*, too. A bruise was already forming on her right cheek, her eye nearly swollen shut. A thin line of blood leaked from her mouth.

In what had become instinct, Nina's hand fell to the curved grip of her Colt. Her jaws locked tight. "I'll kill him."

"No, you won't," Jasmine answered.

"He hit you because of me," Nina tried to keep her voice down, but it threatened to rise. "Because I gave him a little of his own medicine."

Nina started to get up but Jasmine grabbed her arm. "It wasn't because of you."

"What do you mean?"

"He did it because I laughed at him." Jasmine smiled, then grimaced. Nina noticed the tooth just behind her upper incisor had been knocked out, leaving a bloody gap. Jasmine touched her face. "Hurts like hell, but it was worth it."

Nina held up her finger. "The only way it would be worth it is if we put a bullet in his pecker."

Jasmine stared at Nina for a second, and then erupted in laughter. Nina *wanted* to laugh, too, but couldn't get past Jasmine's swollen, purple cheek.

"I spit my tooth in the bucket while he was pullin' his pants up." Jasmine grinned again, eyes filled with mirth.

This time Nina couldn't resist. Thinking of Strobridge drinking several cups of water before discovering the bloody tooth bouncing around the bottom was too much for her to bear. They giggled together, Jasmine simultaneously snickering and crying while Nina's insides wound as tight as a spring.

Jasmine pointed, and Nina followed her finger to find Manning, Buck, and Red Thunder staring at them with puzzled expressions, providing fuel for yet another bout of strained laughter. Just when Nina thought her face might get stuck, their joy subsided. Nina's chest and stomach unclenched, and it seemed like a weight had been lifted from her shoulders.

"You are a wicked thing," she told Jasmine.

"Wicked is all I know."

"If he lays another hand on either of us, I'm going to kill him."

Jasmine nodded.

"I will," she said.

"I don't doubt you, hon."

At that moment, Strobridge walked into No Man's Land accompanied by the Daggetts. At first, Nina thought the tooth had been found and Strobridge wanted more blood, but he was calling amicably for everyone to come to the center, waving them in.

"Injuns welcome, too," he said, smiling that shit-eating grin of his. "Injun *women*, as well."

Pa shifted beside her. "What's that?"

"They're having a meeting."

"I have a feeling…" Pa's eyes became distant, as if looking at something very far away.

"What is it, Pa?" She helped him up. He was still unable to put much weight on his foot, but she had to admit it looked a little better.

Pa shook his head. "Oh, just a feeling like we're nearing the end of something big."

In No Man's Land, Marshal Oden and the priest were already trying to placate Strobridge and the Daggetts.

"Now, James, you know it's sure death if we go out there."

"We don't know that, Mathias. Don't know that at all. Never got the whole story from that Injun girl."

"Yeah, we were a little preoccupied with that talkin' fuckin' corpse," George Daggett added, meaning Grover, much to the dismay of the Buell women.

"Her name is Nina," Pa said, leaning into Nina a bit.

"Whatever. *Nina*," George said. "You see anythin' interesting from the roof? Any way through?"

Nina told them what she saw; silent deaduns packed

inside the fort walls, completely surrounding the building. She related the part about Yellow Hood, how she'd tried to shoot him and what the shambling corpses had done to protect him.

Mathias nodded. "That would be Liao."

Mason Daggett scratched his head. "If that was him out there, then what was that with Grover?"

Manning heaved a sigh. "Haven't you boys figured this out yet? The dead are walking. Devils are possessing people, you get it?"

"That's right," Father Mathias said. "It's certainly a dark, dark time. Souls being purged, balances tilted."

Nina's thoughts lingered on Father Mathias's words, while the rest of them argued some more. She barely caught any of the conversation, but the gist was that Strobridge wanted to leave and Mathias wanted to stay. She couldn't blame Strobridge, not after Liao found out he had this Taiping Jing. All Nina could think about were the legions of dead, mindless, yet somehow still linked with friends and family, fellow workers, too. Whatever seemed familiar to them. It couldn't be a coincidence.

"They must know who they are," she mumbled.

"What?"

Nina cleared her throat. "The deaduns out there. They're families, friends, still together. People who look like they might have known one another before. It's like they're still people in those rotten skulls somewhere."

"Dealing with damnation the only way they can," her pa added.

Father Mathias raised his hands just a little. "While there may be a shadow of the person remaining, trust me when I say their souls are gone."

"How do you know all this shit?" George Daggett seemed to be having real difficulty fully grasping what was happening.

Father Mathias sat down in a nearby chair. "Liao Xu possessed our unfortunate brother, Mister Buell, and spoke through him. Liao is very old. Older than you can imagine, and he's been plotting what he calls the *Great Peace* since before I was born."

"Some peace," Marshal Oden said. "Why here? Why us?"

"Fair question, Marshal. The answer is ill luck."

"Ill fuckin' luck?" George Daggett scratched his head.

"Yes, you see, beneath the surface of everything around you lies a world of darkness and mystery…some might say magic. Life is comprised of good and evil and everything in between. So, the world has not *suddenly* gone bad. It has *always* had the potential to be so. And it has done so before, in olden times."

"Olden…?" George looked damned near about to have another fit. "What the fuck does any of this have to do with us?"

Father Mathias shifted in his chair. "My order, among others, has kept the balance for centuries. Certainly, the scales have tipped back and forth from time to time. Lately, we've been trying to stop Liao Xu. We caught up to him in San Francisco where I was able to take from him the artifact we spoke of earlier. Your Mister Strobridge returned the favor, stealing it from me, and so we're forced to confront both parties here. So, my dear Mister Daggett, you being here is the only coincidence. The rest is quite planned. But I, for one, am glad to have you."

"Glad to…? Well, this all fuckin' figures," George said.

"Indeed it does fucking figure, good George," the priest said in an odd mockery of George's wont to cuss. "And the truth is we're not sure Liao Xu can control what he has unleashed. The soulless husks of humanity, mindless bodies ravenous for flesh."

"Those poor, poor, bastards," Pa said.

"What the fuck you talkin' about?" George looked at Nina's father.

"They were people once, you fool. People with lives and families."

"That's what I'm sayin'." Strobridge's dark, serious eyes checked everyone in the group and settled on Mathias. "That's why we got to make a break for it now, Thomas. So we don't end up like them. Look, I know you hate me, and I'm not too fond of you neither, but you gotta see the sense in us hightailing it outta here."

"Just how do you propose attacking hundreds of these things?" Marshal Oden crossed his massive arms, his bloody shirt ready to burst at the seams.

"My man Woodie'll blast a path through. Everyone else can pick off the strays."

Manning gestured toward Over There. "You mentioned not leaving anyone behind before. What about now? We've got a young girl and a man who can hardly walk. How do you propose to roll the wheelbarrow through all that mess?

Mister Strobridge clenched his jaw. "I was gonna ask you and the marshal to do body patrol. You can clear a path easy enough, at least until we get outside the fort."

"Very well thought out, Mister Strobridge," Mathias nodded, crossing his legs and running his hand over his chin. "But then where will you go? Down to the creek? Hop on a ferry?"

"For your information," Strobridge turned on Mathias. "I've got a *train* prepped for a return east. It was scheduled to start its run today. If we can get to it, we can have it moving inside two hours."

"That's good news, Mister Strobridge, good news. But that train will do you no good. Liao's undead won't stop here. They'll continue east as well, devouring everyone they come across."

"Devouring the land," Red Thunder spoke from somewhere behind them.

Mathias nodded. "Liao must be stopped. Here. Now."

Strobridge growled. "If that bastard Liao dies in the fighting, then so be it. But we can't stay here, holed up in this place with no food, sleeping in our own shit."

"That's right," added Mason.

Strobridge's eyes slid to Manning. "What do you say, son? There's a pretty penny in it for you if you want in."

Manning fixed the railroad boss with his steel stare, hands loosely at his hips, poised above those deadly dragoons. "I'd love to see you go, Mister Strobridge. Hell, you and your idiot nearly got us killed twice already. The two of you have been more of a pain in the ass than any of us want to deal with, but since you have this thing Liao wants, this Taiping Jing, then I can't see why you'd want to go runnin' around drawin' attention to yourselves. Why don't you stay and help us kill Liao?" Manning shrugged. "Then we go for the train."

Mister Strobridge slapped his hand against his leg. "Lily-fuckin'-livers, the damned lot of you."

Mathias shook his head, trying to drive Strobridge to wisdom. "You can't protect the Taiping Jing. If you leave here, you'll be giving Liao what he wants, and it will only enable him to reap and reap and further reap. We can't allow that to happen."

"You saying we *can't* leave?"

"Yes, Mister Strobridge."

"What?"

"We're not letting you leave."

"Nobody and I mean nobody tells J.H. Strobridge what he can and cannot do." The railroad boss slowly turned, sneering, his eyes full of contempt. "Come on, men. We have plans to make."

"You need to turn over your weapons," Marshal Oden said at their backs.

"Fuck *you*," came George Daggett's reply. "Come take 'em."

Oden gave Mathias an uncertain look. Nobody wanted to forcefully disarm the Daggetts.

The priest shook his head and waved dismissively. "Leave them be for now. They'll stew, but they'll come around. There's really no other choice."

Her pa wiped his arm across his sweaty brow. "Not so sure about that, Father. Strobridge has them pretty convinced."

"It'll be fine, Mister Weaver," Mathias replied, although his anxious jaw rubbing told Nina he wasn't so sure either.

CHAPTER TWELVE

R ACHEL BUELL'S SINGSONG MEWLING floated eerily in
the chilly afternoon air. The sound caught Nina's
attention and she looked over where the Buell women sat
on the floor against the wall. Clara stared at nothing and
absently stroked Rachel's hair, the girl laying her head in
her ma's lap. They had been like that since Grover's bodily
destruction.

Nina felt sympathy for both, all-too-familiar with the
sudden and violent loss of a loved one. She worried for
both women's sanity.

Nina knelt before the fire, slowly feeding herself from
a handful of nuts and dried fruit Red Thunder had given
her. Time dragged by, tension thick all around. She watched
Strobridge's gang sulking Over There, milling around in a

cloud of black intent. Being told what to do hadn't sat well
with any of them. Nina hoped the amount of firepower on
this side of the building would keep them in check.

Buck and Red Thunder walked the perimeter. The
roughrider occasionally peered out through a gap in the
barricade. He'd spit, shake his head, and move on, only to
return a moment later and repeat the process.

Mathias had finally given up his seat in No Man's Land
and taken to the floor closer to the fire, where he'd put his
head on his folded robe and pulled a hat over his eyes to
rest. Marshal Oden had taken up one of the chairs in No
Man's Land, facing the barricaded front door. He lounged,
his feet kicked forward, hat tugged low. He sneaked an
occasional glance Over There, keeping tabs on Strobridge
and his lickspittles.

Otherwise, the day passed in nervous anticipation of
what would happen when Liao came calling tomorrow.
No one could deny his control of the situation, a thousand
deaduns surrounding their building and no way to escape.
How could Mathias protect them when their guns and
bombs failed?

"I got a good feeling about Father Mathias," Pa said.

"I'm not sure how you could have a good feeling about
anything, Pa."

"It's all relative, Nina girl."

"Relative to what?" Manning prodded the fire, staring
into it as if their answers lie somewhere within the flames.
He had a whiskey bottle full of water and held it out to
Clara Buell without looking. The woman just stared and
rubbed her sniffling daughter's head, and Manning peered
at them, then set the bottle down by Clara's leg.

"Y'all know what I mean. I'm trying to make the best of the situation," Pa said. "I happen to believe strongly in the Lord. So, either you've not accepted the Lord's presence within yourself, or you just flat out don't like the man."

Manning pulled a crooked grin, which could have been amusement or affirmation. Nina didn't know which. "I never said I didn't like the priest. Followed his lead this morning, didn't I?"

"That you did."

"Just not sure what we're gonna do when those things come pourin' in here in the hundreds."

"I think we all know what's gonna happen." Clara Buell spoke up. The woman looked at them, her eyes suddenly focused albeit haunted. "We're gonna die horribly, and there's nothin' any of us can do about it." She put her hand over Rachel's ear, looked askance. "Would be kind if one of y'all would hand me your piece so I can ensure Rachel's peaceful passage. When the time comes, of course."

No one replied, and Clara looked annoyed. "I know how to use one. Shot vermin back on the farm with my daddy's six shooter, and I can handle a shotgun just fine."

Manning nodded. "When the time comes, Miss, I'll oblige you one of mine."

Satisfied, Clara nodded. "Thank you."

They sat in silence. Jasmine came over and bent down, offering Clara a wet rag. The woman used it to wipe her daughter's dirty face and hair. The woman fussed with pursed lips, showing the forward determination of someone who had accepted their fate with a certain amount of dignity. She thought Ma would have been the same way, only Ma would have had them join hands in a circle while chanting to their guardian spirits; ever faithful to her religion, and peace, in the wake of chaos and death. Was that strength?

"I had a dream," Nina blurted out. Before anyone could reply, she told them about it. The gist of it anyway—words couldn't describe the feeling she'd had being amongst the Shoshone again. She didn't know why, but it seemed important to let them all know that *someone* was protecting them; and maybe to convince herself, too.

When she mentioned the shaman's words about Ma, her pa's head sunk.

"That's an awful nice dream, Nina," he said, "and reminds me of some great memories. Thank you for helping me see what's important right now. Truth be told, I ain't opposed to moving on from this world so I can meet your ma in the next, but I'd never leave you, girl. Not now." Pa reached out and touched her cheek, his skin rough and worn; the hand of a man who never sat idle.

Nina covered his hand with hers. "Don't talk like that, Pa. Thing is, I believe it...that Ma's watchin' over us, I mean." The revelation wasn't a total surprise, but it felt good to recognize it. "Or maybe I just miss her a lot."

Pa looked worn, physically and emotionally. Not surprising given his age, but worrying all the same. Lately, on the trail, he'd needed Nina to take extra time on chores while he rested. Nina hadn't minded. She knew his scout's life had taken a toll on him, and it was hard to imagine how he felt right now, foot all twisted up, and the stress of the past twenty-four hours weighing heavy on him. "I choose to believe it, too."

Nina leaned and wrapped her arms around her father,

squeezing as hard as she dared, sparing a few tears. She couldn't help but think this might be the last time she hugged Pa. No, she had to push those kinds of thoughts away. Weren't nothing but distractions.

Miss Buell—now *widow* Buell—was suddenly standing there, wringing the cloth in her bony hands. She seemed to want to say something, fighting to find the right words. She finally sighed and came out with it. "Just so you know, when we first came here, we weren't…we didn't have no ill feelin's toward y'all or your *kind*. My husband, he was just tryin' to protect us. It's hard to know who to trust these days."

"You sure picked the wrong ones then."

"Nina," Pa chastised.

Clara's smile dripped bitterness. "No, she's right. It was a bad decision. I know that now. And I'm sorry. *We're* sorry."

"Why you tellin' me this?"

"Because I want to make peace with God before we go. And make no mistake, we're *going*." Clara frowned and wrinkled her brow. "And because it was wrong. Grover was a good man and got along with just about anyone. I guess seeing…seeing Mister Thunder there was frightening at first, what with all the raids and the violence these days. I just regret we couldn't have met under better circumstances."

Nina nodded, unsure how to take that. She'd never been good at receiving compliments or apologies. "Never know, Miss Buell. We might make it out of this yet. How'd you end up in those woods anyway?"

Clara told them how they'd been closing up the boot shop for the day, when the deaduns overran the town. A chill ran up Nina's spine as she told how the first ones had simply stood out front, staring in through the windows as if waiting for something.

"Of course, Grover grabbed the shotgun and sent me and Rachel to the back. But we didn't go. We stood there while those things looked in at us. At first, I thought it was a gang of some sort. Like I said, it's wild out here. Don't know who to trust or where you're safe. I told Grover we shoulda never come..." Clara turned her head to the fire, looking through the flames into some other world. "When they busted the front window and tore the front door off its hinges, the smell coming off them was the first thing that hit us. That's when we knew exactly what they were. It didn't take but a second more to realize it was the end of days. Just like the good book says."

"I know how you feel, Miss Buell," Nina said. "Me and Pa—"

"Grover blew a hole in one of 'em, getting guts all over the new high work leathers we got in just last week," Miss Buell went on like Nina hadn't even spoken. "I remember putting those out and thinking Grover was asking too much. They weren't the same company we usually got 'em from. Shoddy." She laughed. "Now maybe he'll let me mark 'em down."

Nina laughed uncomfortably along with her. "I reckon you could have a bloody boot sale."

Clara beamed, wiping a lock of wispy brown hair from her eyes. "Yes, indeed."

"What happened then?" Manning regarded the widow with those intent eyes of his as he nibbled.

Glad to have her attention taken, Nina admired James Manning, unabashedly. No sense in being shy about it anymore, not if they were all a hair's breadth from Hell.

Her eyes traced the strands of sweat-greasy hair poking out from beneath his hat, down to his ears and then along his unshaved jawline. Two or three day's growth on his face only made him that much more attractive. Her heart beat faster, and she resisted the urge to reach out and touch him.

Did he feel the same way? She had an inkling, but the uncertainty was all that stopped her.

Truth was she'd never thought about men much before. Well, maybe on some nights she'd dreamed about the young Indian fellas she'd met in their visits to the tribe. Copper skin rubbing against hers as they rolled in the grass beneath the full moon. But she'd certainly never felt anything this strong…this close. It was strange after what she'd imagined with Jasmine.

She found herself wishing the same thing as Clara Buell, only different; that she'd met James Manning under much better circumstances. But what then? Would Nina have thought him just another rough man in a rough world? Would she have felt the strength of his touch or seen the compassion in his eyes? Nina liked everything about him, even though she'd failed to admit it before. This time, when he caught her staring, Nina didn't look away.

"Grover shooed us out back where we already had the pony hitched. Bacon was barking his head off. We jumped in the back and started down the trail to…I'm not sure where we were going, exactly. Home, I suppose. We live not quite a mile outside town. Lot of good that would have done us, though. Getting home.

"Anyway, more of them things came out of the woods and spooked the pony. Grover couldn't keep him on the trail and we ended up hitting a tree, right where you found us. They got the animals first. Poor Bacon, trying to protect us. He'd been Grover's dog. When Grover saw one of them things pick up Bacon and bite him, he went crazy. I never saw that man so mad in his life. I was proud of him for fending those things off. And, well, you know the rest."

"Sorry about Grover, ma'am." Manning tipped his hat to her.

"Oh, it's not your fault. Can't no one stop God when he wants somethin' done."

Nina harrumphed. "Well, if God is doing all this, let's hope he takes a nap soon. We could use a damn break."

"It's hard to keep one's faith," Clara said, shifting so she rested on her heels. Her eyes raised as if she expected Grover to come walking over any second. "But at the same time, I welcome this." She waved a hand indicating everything. "The dead folk walking, and the demon who took my husband...the end of the world. It only proves to me that God is real, too. He *has* to be." Her expression changed to curiosity. "I wonder what Mister George Daggett wants?"

"No good, no doubt," Manning said, standing as the group turned to look at Mean George coming their way.

He strode over with an exaggerated swagger, thumbs in his belt loops as if he were strolling through a field of daisies. The loud-mouthed bastard appeared to be weaponless, yet still wore an air of cockiness only a truly ignorant man could pull off.

Marshal Oden was waiting for him with crossed arms. Instead of stopping in front of the marshal, George tried to slide on past. Oden caught him by the arm. "Where do you think you're goin'?"

"Just want some water," George said, still trying to squeeze past.

"What's your trade, son?"

"We ain't got nothin' more to fuckin' trade. You done took all our whiskey. You got all the women now, too."

"You got *somethin'*."

George backed up, so Oden let him go. The Daggett dipped his head and brought it up shaking, looking provoked. "We ain't givin' over our guns, you hear?"

"You can't drink black powder, either."

"Oh, that's funny."

"Wasn't meant to be."

"Look, you gonna let us die of thirst over there? You call yourself a man of justice?"

"Trade us your Spencers, and you can have all the water you want."

"You'd disarm us with all those fuckin' deaduns out there?"

"You can have 'em back if we're attacked."

George dragged a hand down his face. "Aw, fuck it. I never did get along with you lawdogs anyway." With that, he produced a short blade and stabbed Marshal Oden in the gut.

CHAPTER THIRTEEN

MARSHAL ODEN CLUTCHED HIS belly, staggering back before George could get in another poke. A dark cloud passed over the Marshal's face. He glanced at George's little knife and growled. With surprising speed, the big guy cocked his meaty arm and lunged.

George was quick, partially blocking Oden's swing, receiving a glancing blow to the cheek that was still enough to put him on his ass.

Everyone drew, Nina included, and that's when she realized their mistake. Mister Strobridge, Woodie, and Mason had dragged a patchwork shield made from pieces of wood into No Man's Land and hunkered behind it, protected near the far wall where Grover's remains were covered by a tattered blanket.

George rolled in behind them, and Strobridge shouted, "Now!"

Woodie tossed one of his damned balls over the shield.

Nina had about a second to wonder how they hadn't seen this coming, before the world vomited light and sound. She was thrown across the room and struck the wall, jarring the breath from her body. She landed hard on her tailbone as the sky winked repeatedly, fragments of wood pummeling her, her vision obscured by dust and smoke. Something sharp gouged her shoulder and she curled up as best she could, covering her head until the worst was over.

Beneath the dwindling sounds of falling debris came a low rumble. The ground shifted. The wall at her back moved. Knowing she could be brained by dropping stones, Nina scrambled, panic-crazed, to get out from under the pile of debris. She kicked her legs free, shoved several large, heavy timbers off her head, choking on dirt and bits of wood as she tried to catch her breath.

Once free, Nina looked for Pa and found him crawling toward her. He was covered in dust and shouting something, but Nina's ears were ringing. She couldn't hear a dern thing. She waved her hand to indicate she was okay and crawled away from the quaking wall.

She shifted her hat and peered around through the haze as the ground continued to rumble. Red Thunder had fallen across the fire holes and was rolling clear of the flames. Buck sat on the ground, howling and holding his knee, blood blossoming in his pants leg.

Over There, the far wall was gone. A score of deaduns were scattered and blown to pieces outside. Strobridge and the Daggetts threw down their wooden shield, pulled pieces of cloth from their ears, and ran for the new opening, weapons blazing. Woodie scuttled behind them, carrying an extra sack over his shoulder. It looked as if they'd tied together several shirts and put the remaining ammunition inside.

Nina went to draw on the bastards, hoping to get at least one of them, then realized her Colt was gone. She'd been holding it when the bomb went off. Her eyes scanned the dirt floor and spied it lying on the edge of No Man's Land, several yards away. She wanted to go get it, but couldn't seem to make her body move. She could barely see anything above the cloud of dust and dirt whipping around.

A sudden crack split the ground with a vibration like thunder, fractures splicing beneath them. Without thinking, Nina grasped Pa's outstretched arms and yanked as a massive slab of floor bucked and collapsed completely, taking Red Thunder with it. Buck flipped and started to slide in, but at the last second latched hold of the edge and crawled from the brink.

Pa covered Nina as they hunkered against the wavering wall. She was fearful it might collapse but was also afraid of being dumped into the darkness. She reached out and put her hand against the vibrating stone, as if she could hold the damn thing up. More of the roof fell in, sharp things nipping her exposed skin. Pa cursed and held her tight.

Just as quickly as it started, the rumbling stopped, leaving nothing but silence and the leftover drone in her head.

In the distance, shots rang out.

Someone groaned nearby. A man called out, maybe Manning, she couldn't be sure. For the second time, she and her pa unburied themselves, pushing off rotted wood. She pulled Pa to his knees and inspected the damage.

They were on the precipice of a hole that had to be twelve or fifteen feet deep and about ten feet wide. The slab of floor that had fallen in was partially lit by the gray sky, but there was no sign of Red Thunder, and Nina felt sad about that, but there was no time to dwell.

The fissure undercut the well walls, which had also collapsed inward, burying the water hole for good. Another crack had broken the floor of No Man's Land, and the priest and the marshal stood amidst the partially crumbled roof and walls. Oden's hand covered the red stain on his abdomen where George had stabbed him and he grimaced.

The man who'd been calling out to her *was* Manning. She turned her head to see him trying to work his way around the fissure to her left. Cuts lined his face, but she saw the urgency in his eyes. He held his hands out, palms up. "Stay there!"

Nina nodded, but she didn't think he could make it to her. There was only one or two feet between the wall and sinkhole, and much of that was blocked by debris. The front doors had collapsed in and lay across the rubble, and she could see the deaduns outside coming to life.

Somewhere to her left, Jasmine was yelling as she dug around in the debris, trying to find Clara and Rachel.

"My gun," Nina said to Manning, her voice sounding loud in her head.

"What?"

Nina realized she'd hardly made a noise. "Throw my gun," she shouted, her voice like a cannon in her head, adding to the splitting headache already there. She pointed at the weapon for good measure.

Manning nodded and went over, picked it up, and blew the dust off. He turned it around, gripped it by the top, and tossed it over. Nina's hands came to life, snatching it out of the air. She checked the caps and load. Everything *looked* okay. She just hoped the damn thing still fired.

Pa put his hand on her shoulder, leaning on her some while balancing on one foot. "You okay?"

"I think so. You?"

"I'm going to *have* to be okay, girl. I'll limp, crawl, or shuffle my way around. Just doesn't look like there's any place to go."

Nina glanced at Jasmine, who'd managed to get the debris off Clara Buell.

The deaduns were riled up, gnashing with those trap jaws, flexing rotted fists. Yet, they didn't come. Maybe Liao, or God, or who-the-fuck-ever, was indeed taking a nap.

Jasmine made a fearful noise, her hand clamping over her mouth as she scooted away from Clara Buell.

"What is it?"

Jasmine shook her head, getting as far away as she could without falling into the hole.

"Pa?"

"Go on and help her. I can stand here until those boys find a way to get me across."

Nina left him leaning against the wall and picked her way over to Jasmine.

"What is…"

One look at Clara Buell and Nina understood. The woman sprawled atop a pile of wood where Jasmine had rolled her over, one bony leg dangling out over the precipice.

At first glance, Clara looked dead. Nina *hoped* she was because a flat piece of rock had wedged itself horizontally into her eye socket. The ruined eyeball oozed around the stone, blood running out the sides in rivulets. The injury might not kill her right away, but it would hurt like hell. And who knew how a wound like that might fester without immediate attention? Nina gripped her Colt and thought about putting it to use on Clara, remembering Manning's promise to the woman.

Clara Buell gasped and woke up, her good eye working in a flurry of blinks. She glared at Jasmine, and then Nina. Her wounded eye tried to work but managed only to twitch and wiggle around the rock. "Where's Rachel?" Her calm tone belied her condition.

Nina went down on her knee next to Clara, the wound looking even worse close up. She tried not to stare. "Rachel's okay. Right, Jasmine?"

"She's here." That much was true. Jasmine had helped Rachel up and pulled the girl into her arms.

Clara smiled, reaching toward her weeping daughter. "Oh, thank you so much." She shook her head. "What happened? I remember that awful Daggett and then an explosion...oh, I don't feel so well."

She looked much worse than not well, but they needed to get moving. Rachel tried to look at her mother, but Jasmine embraced her tight, pulling her head away.

Clara's face filled with confusion, her good eye darting around as if she just now sensed something wrong. She drew a sudden, sharp intake of breath and said, "Ow."

Nina took the woman's arm, coaxing her up. "We need to get over to the other side of this hole, Clara. The deaduns will be coming soon…see the hole?"

Clara jerked her hand away and put it over her eye socket. "What's this?" She felt the stone's sharp edge, then pressed her fingers lightly against her brow, touching her temple and cheek. "What…" A high, thin whine began in Clara's throat as the pain registered. A drawn out "nooo" joined the whine.

Nina tried to touch her, to console her somehow, but Clara wouldn't have it. With each consecutive breath, the woman got louder, her whines swelling into full-breathed howls. She picked at the rock with a shaking hand, but it wouldn't budge, the gelatinous composition of her eye suctioned around it.

Nina grabbed Clara's hand. "Clara…don't…you can't pull it out. Don't…" Nina fought with the woman, who slapped Nina back, her open hands turning into fists. Nina caught a shot to the head, but snagged Clara's wrist, grunting as she pulled it down.

What Nina didn't anticipate was the woman's left cross to her jaw. The punch rattled her teeth and sent her brain spinning. A guttural snort burst from her lips, and she raised her pistol over her head and slammed it down.

Clara fell limp on a pile of rot-musty wood.

"Ma? Ma!" Rachel squirmed in Jasmine's arms, nearly knocking them both into the pit.

Nina snatched Rachel's arm, yanked her from Jasmine's grasp, and spun her around to face her. "Look here now…" She paused a sec, glanced to see that Manning and the priest had placed a large beam across the pit, Mathias balancing carefully across it.

Rachel squirmed and screamed in a shuffle of rage and

frustration. Nina squeezed the girl's arm, shook her some. "Rachel Buell, listen to me. Listen!"

The girl stopped and stared at Nina.

"Your mother is very ill, and she's sleeping. We're going to get her to a doctor as soon as we can, but we need you to grow the hell up quick. Can you do that for me?"

This was rough treatment, Nina knew it. She reckoned Rachel was about the same age she was when she lost her ma. Pa had done the same for her when she'd caterwauled in hysterics on that terrible day.

The girl squeezed her eyes shut, a stream of tears spilling out from the cracks, and nodded. "Is my mama going to die?"

It was a fair question.

"I won't lie. She's hurt real bad..." Nina clutched Rachel's shoulder. "There's a real good possibility she might die. But if you calm down and help us, your Ma's got a lot better chance. You just need to..." Rachel had stopped paying attention, the girl's eyes drifting up, tracing something behind her. The light from the dead gray sky reflected something there, something rising...something huge.

She looked aside, saw Jasmine, Manning, and Mathias peering up behind her as well, all of them round-eyed and slack-jawed.

"Christ..." Manning said in a drawn-out whisper.

"Christ indeed," echoed Father Mathias. "Saints help us."

CHAPTER FOURTEEN

N INA SHIFTED TO FACE this new terror, her pistol raised. When she saw it, her knees nea rly buckled, heart thumping in her chest. Only her hand against the wall kept her from collapsing. But what would keep her from going insane? What would keep her from losing her goddamn mind and ending up a gibbering mess?

Two spindly, insect limbs as thick as tree branches hooked the top of the wall and pulled it down in a tumble of rock. A fat, bulbous torso fell upon the ruins, followed by two more legs tipped with hooked talons. Several long, wavering tentacles, the color of rancid meat, rolled from its thorax and probed the ground. Its hoary coat was the color of charcoal, plates of tin and steel sparsely woven into the hide.

Wings unfurled, a pattern of black and gray swirls to match the sky at its back.

It wore a mask of bone, mouth a vertical slit filled with large, human-like teeth, eyes the same bulging black Grover Buell's had been. Feathery antennae sprouted from its head.

Liao's voice poured out of that gnashing mouth, his tone a snide elegance that flowed in defiance of the creature's deformed maw. "I dreamt I was a butterfly, but when I awoke, I wondered if it was the butterfly dreaming of me." The thing laughed, its monstrous body quaking with the sound.

The smell of dead flowers was overpowering. More like a *garden* of dead flowers; the sweet decay of leaf, stem, and withered root.

Liao's eyes locked on Jasmine where she'd fallen across a pile of rubble, paralyzed with fear. Two foul tentacles slithered along the ruins toward her. Nina holstered her weapon and drew her blade. Against all instincts, she picked her way over the debris, stepping across a panel of wooden shingles to stoop over her friend.

"No!" Jasmine screamed, just before the tentacles leapt forward, wrapping around her legs with a moist hiss.

Nina poised to strike, but a bright light flushed the air, a powdery luminescence that eased her fear. She looked over her shoulder to see Father Mathias still standing on the beam across the hole, holding up a small crucifix between his index finger and thumb.

"Hold, beast!"

The foul creature reared up, twisting, its spindly arms thrown up in a weak attempt to block Mathias's holy light. The wings curled, quivering. The tentacles held Jasmine a moment more, then released her, slithering away with desperate insistence.

"You're wasting your time on us, Liao. Strobridge has what you want."

The thing that was Liao squinted and winced before keening at the light. "My heavenly subjects will bring Mister Strobridge to me. In the meantime, I thought I would take the opportunity to rid myself of some pests."

"Do pests fight back, Liao?" Mathias spat the words and raised his cross higher, pressing the beam of light against the creature's skin, smoldering it in wisps of smoke.

"Some pests bite but, in the end, they are easily stamped out." Liao's claws anchored him to the walls and earth. His massive wings spread, beating the air with frantic thrusts. The foul scent of dead flowers rose once more, riding on the tails of a buffeting wind. The scent filled Nina's head, reminding her of death. Once again her spirits sank.

The tentacles returned, yanking Jasmine off the pile of rubble.

Nina leapt into action, her fears trounced by desperation. She clutched one tentacle, sawing at it with her knife. It was icy to the touch, strong and sinuous. It jerked Jasmine out of reach.

Nina leapt and fell atop the woman to keep her from moving and started sawing again. One more cut and the horrid appendage was severed, waving around and shooting gouts of oily black ichor everywhere.

The other tentacle released its hold and swatted Nina across the face. Her head rang, but she managed to shield herself with her arm long enough to crawl over Jasmine and get to her feet. Once up, Nina ducked a wild swipe, narrowly avoiding being knocked into the pit.

She thought she heard Pa yelling for her just before gunshots rang out. Wings batted the air, stirring up a cloud of dust and darkness that battled Mathias's white force. A fist-sized rock struck Liao in the face, bouncing harmlessly away. In return, two clawed legs ripped apart a section of crumbling wall and hurtled the mess across the pit.

The tentacle stalked Nina, hovering before her, feinting. It was so fast she could barely track its movement. She held her blade point up, swinging at every movement. She might have nicked it once or twice.

Nina switched her stance, one misplaced foot twisting on a rock. The tentacle dove in, the tip poking her in the stomach. Her counter slice just missed the retreating appendage. Before she could blink, it thrust again, this time drilling her in the left shoulder, sending her flying to the ground.

Nina tried to move, but the thing was on her, beating her relentlessly while more tentacles slid past to get at the others. She heard Jasmine grunt and yell repeatedly, gutturally, as she attempted to fight off the invading swarm. Rachel Buell screamed a cry of terror that drove Nina on.

She kicked and swung wildly, her own voice lending urgency to the fight.

The sound of drums sounded faintly in the back of her mind, a slow, steady rhythm in all the chaos. Time slowed, her focus narrowed, tired arms found strength. The crafty appendage stood out in vivid clarity.

Nina let it come.

When it struck, she caught the tendril with her left arm, wrapping it up in a tight grip. It yanked her from the ground, pulling her forward. She angled her feet, but missed the landing; instead, Nina struck the pile of wood-jagged debris chest first. The wind rushed from her lungs, yet she hung on.

"Die, fucker, die!" Nina sawed the appendage until it snapped loose, trailing away in spouts of murky blood. She crawled to her knees, her body shaking, lungs so sore it almost wasn't worth it to breathe. More shots rang out, but she hardly cared. *Just a minute to rest, twenty seconds even.*

Rachel Buell slid by too fast for Nina to react, dragged by one of those things. She made a silent apology, her heart breaking, as the girl was lifted into the air, out of reach.

Father Mathias saw it, too. "Unhand that servant of the Lord, foul beast. Creature of Hell! It is *God* who commands you!"

But Liao's dark power saturated the air, his foul reek permeating everything. Two of his clawed feet were busy with Manning and Marshal Oden while his eyes remained locked on the Father Mathias. "It's over, Thomas!"

Clara Buell felt otherwise.

The woman charged over Nina, teeth bared as she hooked her arms around the thieving vine. Clara's damaged eye leaked down the side of her face, unable to remain in her head any longer. The Liao beast lifted her, kicking and screaming, into the air. She opened her mouth and clamped down on the tough, fibrous appendage, head tearing back and forth like a vicious dog.

The thing's grasp on Rachel loosened, and Nina saw her chance, reaching over the emptiness to pull the girl in. Two more of the snaky tendrils wrapped themselves around Clara's body. The three together slammed her to the jagged ground. Still, the mad woman clung. Her face was covered in gore as she gnawed, finally pulling the two pieces apart in a cry of victory.

She held the squirming tendril over her head and whooped, only to be squeezed unmercifully and ripped apart. Everything inside her poured out; intestines, organs, and what seemed like buckets of blood. Liao Xu tossed Clara's halves away.

Rachel Buell let loose an anguished, shrill sound as Liao pulled his massive bulk over the pile of crushed stone, his wings moving lazily as he searched for his next victim.

Nina hugged Rachel close and offered what she could in the last minutes of their lives; the feel of a human embrace. She looked across at her pa, where he was slumped against a tumbled pile of timber and clay bricks. He looked back, eyes wet, and gave her a serene nod, reached up with a bloodied hand and blew his daughter a final kiss.

"That's it," Nina whispered in Rachel's ear. "But it's okay…" She could hardly believe it. It was her time, *everyone's* time, and she'd pass into the next world along with Pa, Manning, and Jasmine. Rachel, too. Fuck the rest. Maybe Pa was right. Maybe it was better to end it now than to keep on suffering in this shithole of a world.

A war cry shook Nina to the core, the sharp sound sending chills up her spine. She'd heard similar calls when braves returned from a hunt or scouting mission, but this was different. Driven from the lungs of an enraged warrior, it sounded like a death knell to all within earshot.

Red Thunder bounded from the pit and up the slanted slab. He'd stripped away his vest, exposing his coppery skin and muscled torso. His eyes flashed with hatred, his dark hair flying wild behind him. He'd colored the top half of his face with mud or coal, looking like a screaming demon risen from the dark to deal proper justice to his foe.

Tomahawk held high, he charged up the pile of stone and wood and swiped at Liao's masked face. The monstrous visage jerked back, barely avoiding being cleaved in two. Tendrils fell on the warrior, but Red Thunder hacked them to pieces. One found purchase, wrapping around his chest, holding him in place while a clawed leg poised to end the warrior.

As it descended, Marshal Oden was suddenly there, stepping in and catching the dagger-like tip on his shoulder. The marshal wrapped his big arms over the top of the leg as the claw snapped in again, thunking into his back. The big man's cry rang out as he was forced to his knees. Still, he bared his teeth and held on to the appendage for all his worth, bearing down with his prodigious strength and tethering Liao in place.

"Kill…it!" Oden growled through bloodied teeth. The beast thrashed, but the marshal held on, roaring.

Manning yelled and charged up the pile with Nina's ax in hand. He severed the sinuous tendril holding Red Thunder and went to work on the core of clumped, wiggly things. His ax head threw off ropy globs of blackened goop as it rose and fell. Red Thunder spun, dodging another deadly claw, and buried his tomahawk in the thing's side.

Liao's face was too high for them to reach. Except for Buck Patterson. The wounded man had limped halfway up the sliding scree. He raised his weapon, and a fat ball of lead smashed the mask's forehead to pieces, bone-colored shards spinning away like a rain of stars.

Liao squealed, jerking from side-to-side as more of Buck's slugs pounded home. Seeing those fathomless eyes wide with terror was one of the most satisfying things Nina had ever witnessed.

Mathias's holy light grew bright once again. She glanced back to see the priest kneeling on the beam, one shaky hand still holding his cross high, the other fist to his chest as he prayed to his Lord.

Nina staggered to her feet, prepared to charge up the mound if she could. But then the beast shrunk away, by reflex jerking the marshal down before its claw wrenched free. A cloud of dense fog rolled in, covering Liao's retreat.

"Fuck you and the horse you rode in on!" Buck screamed, sending one more shot into the mist, receiving a satisfying squeal in response.

Manning looked down at Nina from the top of the pile, his face a mess of blood and gunk. Nina smiled up at him, feeling giddy. They were *alive*. Well, most of them, anyway.

Marshal Oden's blank, lifeless stare was fixed on Heaven, and Nina sure hoped the big man had made it there.

A few moments later, deaduns moaned from the mist.

They were coming.

CHAPTER FIFTEEN

WHAT DO WE DO now?" Pa asked as Nina got under his arm.

"I swallowed my chaw," Buck announced.

They looked at him. "It was my last plug," the roughrider explained, then winced at his leg.

"I meant what do we do now we're surrounded by the walkin' dead."

"We sure as shit ain't got no ammo. At least nothing for my piece." Buck spun his chamber and holstered his weapon.

"And we have injured," Manning added.

"We go down there." Red Thunder nodded to the pit.

Pa peered over the edge. "Ain't that a drop?"

Red Thunder put his foot out over the gap and stepped

off. Nina gasped but was relieved when the Indian landed just a few feet down, his head clearly visible.

"The way is hidden by shadow. There are some cracks, so we must be careful, but the floor evens out below. Come."

"Must be part of the river that feeds the well," Pa said. "Ain't no tellin' what's down there. Might get ourselves trapped."

"Well, we know what's up here, Lincoln," said Manning.

Pa nodded at that. "Let's go then."

"What about the dead?" Jasmine asked.

"Ain't nothing can be done about it," said Buck. "We'll honor 'em later if we get the chance."

"And pray for their immortal souls," Father Mathias added. "Samuel Oden was a good man and a friend. His place in heaven is assured."

"Come," Red Thunder repeated.

Nina could hear the moans getting louder. Some debris tumbled down from the top of the pile to their right.

She saw Jasmine trying to haul Rachel to her feet, but the girl was staring dumbly at nothing in particular. "Rachel, we have to go," the black woman said.

"Leave me," the girl said. "I want to stay with my ma and pa."

"Your mama gave her life so you could live," Nina said. "Let's go. Deaduns are coming."

"I don't care," Rachel said, still looking at the ground.

Nina marched over. "Get her," she told Jasmine. "We don't have time for this horseshit. You think your pa would want you getting pulled apart and et?"

"Come on," her own pa hissed. He was sitting on the edge of the hole in the floor, looking past them through the dust at the opening in the debris. Shadows were shifting and they had but seconds.

Rachel was a limp doll as Nina and Jasmine pulled her to her feet and led her over. Manning and Red Thunder were helping the others down, and James reached up and took hold of Rachel, as well.

They all made haste down into the darkness. Nina was last and she saw the first deadun tumble down the debris pile and flop into the room.

She ducked down into the hole. The dim light of day extinguished. At first, Nina thought they'd made a good decision, but once down in the dank dark, she wasn't so sure. The black was all-encompassing, and the air had dropped several degrees. "Ain't none of us got a light?" she whispered, feeling squirrelly.

She heard some fussing around, a spark flared, and there was Buck's grinning face surrounded by a halo of illumination from the head of a tiny stick.

"Safety matches. Won two boxes from a feller in Sacramento playing five card stud."

Manning had some ripped up cloth and he wrapped the end of one of the wood slivers with it, while Buck pulled a flask from his back pocket. The roughrider unscrewed the cap, frowned, and poured some whiskey over the fabric. Nina smelled the stuff from where she stood, saliva welling up in her mouth. Anything other than dust and creek water sounded delicious about now.

Before his match went out, Buck lit the makeshift torch to reveal much of what Nina already suspected: wet, dripping walls and a circle of filthy, tired faces.

Something tumbled from above, thumping heavily and

rolling down the slab. They scrambled out of the way as the deadun Nina had spied above skidded to a halt at their feet.

Manning stepped back and buried his ax between its eyes with a *thunk*. He was getting downright deadly with that thing. Nina stared at the corpse's pasty gray skin covered with that odd, flowing script. She should be used to them by now, and maybe part of her was, but questions rose above her fear. *How the hell had it come to be, exactly?* She knew it was Liao Xu, but *how?* She'd have to ask Mathias when she got a chance.

"Okay. Let's get moving," Manning said. "More might be behind this one."

"And I'm sorry to say, despite our small victory, it won't take long for Liao to recover," Father Mathias said. "Although he'll think twice about rushing in so eagerly, or face the Lord's wrath."

Nina gave the priest a sour look.

"Right. He'll probably rush in regardless. Seems a bit maniacal like that," Buck added.

"But only if his *heavenly* subjects find us first," said Manning. "If we can elude them, we might make it."

"We don't have a damn clue where we're going." Nina caught herself *not* using 'god damn' out of respect for Mathias's religion. She recalled Red Thunder's words about faiths and gods being the same across all religions.

"Well, let's go nowhere fast," Manning said.

They shuffled forth, Buck, Mathias, and Manning first; Nina, Pa, and the girls in the middle; and Red Thunder bringing up the rear. Nina fit fine under Pa's shoulder, giving him just enough support to keep off his foot. Pa grunted whenever it bumped something, bare and unprotected as it was. The sound of rushing water always seemed close by, yet somehow distant, too. Nina felt a spike of panic and started to grow faint, her breath coming quick in and out. What if thousands of gallons of water rushed by just feet above their heads? What if the cave collapsed?

She got angry for spookin' herself. After all the mayhem they'd faced, Nina wasn't about to lose all control due to her own dang imagination.

They trudged on, Nina focusing on one step at a time, her stomach nauseated and rumbly. Hell, they were all hungry, but thinking about food was much better than thinking about the tight tunnel, the possibility of running into a dead end, or hundreds of deaduns falling into the hole behind them. *Get a damn grip!*

Pa asked, "What you think happened to Strobridge and his boys, Father?"

"Hopefully dead," Nina muttered.

Pa clicked his tongue. "I'm talkin' to the good Father."

"Hopefully dead," the priest replied over his shoulder.

The floor declined gently, and if Nina remembered Pa's maps correctly, their path would take them down to Maples Creek. It was only maybe a half mile from the fort, give or take, so Nina expected some kind of conclusion soon. Freedom or death. Or maybe this passage went on forever? Pa was starting to get heavy, leaning on her more and more—everyone here had to be past tuckered out.

Nina focused on the light from Buck's torch. She imagined Pa's long stride and her three strides in between forming a rhythm, a rhythm pounded out by Shoshone drums. It wasn't perfect, no, but the percussive sounds soothed her senses, allowing herself to sink into a trance.

A meditative state, her mother would say. Nina had seen Ma do it hundreds of times, but the little girl back then had been perfectly happy playing in the grass and flowers around her silent, still guardian.

A harsh hiss broke through her reveries. Nina's eyes snapped open. Manning was there, peering up the tunnel over her shoulder.

Red Thunder crouched, his attention fixed in the same direction. "Someone's coming."

"Kill the torch," Manning said, "and keep quiet."

The blackness swallowed them, but Nina could see what they meant. Light flickered toward them, the tiniest bit of luminance bouncing off the tunnel walls. Soon, voices could be heard, and it took Nina two seconds to realize who it was. A cold, sickness settled in her guts.

"Pa," she whispered, "I'm going to set you down."

Nina drew her pistol and hunting knife and knelt near Red Thunder. Part of her protested what she was about to do, but it was life or death now, and there were certain people who, by their own goddamn nature, made life a lot more dangerous than necessary. Namely, the no-good bastards working their way down the tunnel.

As they drew closer, shadows danced along the wall where the tunnel curved upward. Strobridge's rangy silhouette came first, limping heavily, followed by the hobbling Les Woodruff, and then the Daggetts.

Nina took a deep breath of cold, musty air and tensed.

Red Thunder's loping form shot past Mister Strobridge and took Mason Daggett down while James Manning's shadow made a direct line for George. Nina took three steps and pointed her gun at Strobridge's head. She caught sight of Woodruff backing up right into Buck, who grabbed him by the scruff of his neck.

"Ow!" George Daggett called out, sounding good and surprised. A scuffle ensued followed by something clattering to the ground. "All right, goddamn it. Alright! I give up."

Mister Strobridge held up his hand, eyeballing the barrel pressed against his cheek. "Darlin', we need to quit finding ourselves in this position."

"This is the only position we'll ever find ourselves in."

Manning stood up in their midst, fists clenched at his sides. "Your plan not work out so well?"

"Ain't got a lot of time to explain ourselves. Deaduns are after us."

"All the more reason to do what needs to be done with you maggots," Nina snarled, shoving her muzzle into Strobridge's hairy cheek.

The boss pushed his face into the Colt's barrel, causing Nina to withdraw the pistol back a little. "I'm the only one who can work that goddamn train," he said, brows lowered. "So you ought not be killin' your only chance of getting the hell outta here," then added with a curl of his lip, "*squaw*."

Manning's steel gaze threatened to cut Strobridge in two. "Fine." Manning turned and laid Woodie out with one punch. Buck let loose of the man as he folded, and Manning fell on top of him to finish the job he'd started the night before. "Finally brought it all fucking down, didn't you?" Each word spat between blows. Even in the near pitch black, Nina could see Woodie's face opening up all over again.

"I got a lot of reasons to kill you," Nina said, pushing the barrel into Strobridge's bearded face, causing him to crane his neck back. "Ain't enough bullets in this gun."

The railroad boss nodded, as if he'd expected this kind of welcome. "We can settle scores later."

Leaving Woodie a sprawling mess, Manning stood, still breathing like a mad bull. "As for you," he said, and snatched Mean George's Spencer off the ground, turned it on him, and pulled the trigger a half-dozen times.

George snickered. "All out."

Manning jammed the barrel of the weapon into George's belly, then he flipped it, took hold of the barrel, and cracked the twisted grin off his face with the stock. George went down, hands up to protect his head.

Mason started to intervene but Red Thunder held the business end of his tomahawk to the rebel's throat.

"Fuck, man! Ease up," George whined, holding his hand to his face.

"Like you eased up on Marshal Oden?" He kicked George in the leg.

"*Fuck*, Manning. I barely hurt the guy. It was a goddamn potato peeler. I knew he'd be fine. We was just tryin' to get out of there. We needed a distraction…"

"It's true." Mason glared at Manning. "Y'all wouldn't let us leave, so we didn't have a choice. *You* made us stab the marshal." He blinked and looked around. "Where is he?"

"Dead." Manning shook his head, his nostrils flaring. The torchlight bathed his face in a hellish glow, and for a moment Nina wondered about their humanity. Were they all losing it? Had they ever *had* it?

"Let's go," she said, pushing away from Strobridge and holstering her Colt. "Come on, Pa."

"Leave them here?" Manning looked at her.

"Yer sick of their gas, I'm sick of their bullshit, and I'm not wasting a bullet to hobble Strobridge here by shooting him in the leg and leaving him for the deaduns."

Manning shook his head. "I don't know. Dangerous leaving them behind."

"Then shoot 'em or bring 'em."

Manning chuckled. "As you please, *Ninataku*."

Nina stopped, looked at Manning, then at Red Thunder, who still had his tomahawk ready to bury in Mason Daggett's skull if it came to it. "You told him my name?" she asked the Indian.

Red Thunder didn't have time to answer, as Manning said, "You were singing in your sleep. The song. There were other words, but that's the one I remembered."

"Oh."

"*Ninataku* means Fire-Eater," her pa explained. "Her Goshute name."

Buck re-lit his torch. "Stay away from this then, Fire-Eater," he said to Nina. "We're plumb outta bug juice."

"How about you not shoot us then and we get to my train?"

"Fine," Manning glowered. "Like you said, we'll reckon things out later."

"Fair enough," Strobridge said.

"Let's scoot," Buck pushed past the group with his light, and Nina took her place beside Pa, and just in front of Jasmine and Rachel, the whites of their eyes shining.

Strobridge and the Daggetts walked in front, just behind Buck, so everyone could keep an eye on them. The Daggets ushered the battered Woodruff between them. The man lurched in a daze, dragging his feet and stumbling often. Mason and George hefted him back to his feet every time, until finally George griped, "Pull it together, man. We ain't got no damn wheelbarrow no more."

Nina wasn't surprised. Footing was treacherous even for those who hadn't just suffered a beat down. The floor was slick in some spots; massive, wet stones set into the packed dirt. 'Neckbreakers' Buck called them, sure to let everyone know whenever he passed one.

Strange, colorless bugs scampered into cracks, frightened by the torchlight. They passed spots where the trickling flow emerged to run straight down the middle of the tunnel, sometimes forcing them to traverse tiny pools of black water.

As they walked, Nina thought about why she hadn't pulled the trigger. Part of her realized she'd probably made a mistake leaving Strobridge alive. The other part thought Ma would be proud. Maybe it was the moment she'd seen Manning as a demon, a man capable of incredible violence. In any case, they were surviving, and that's all that mattered. She put her faith in her decision and left it alone.

Her thoughts were interrupted by Buck's cry. "Light ahead. Woohoo!"

Sure enough, the tunnel became saturated with it as they went. Nina's pace quickened by the idea she and her pa might see the sky one more time before they died. They exited a vertical fissure, squeezing through and coming out the other side into a thick forest at the base of a rise. Nina breathed in the evergreen scents of pine and silver spruce, her head dizzy with delight, the smell of death gone save for the stink of their own garments.

They followed the trickles of water down to Maples Creek, Nina's ears happy to hear something besides black powder explosions and moaning deaduns. Everyone whooped and hollered. Manning even wrapped his arms around Nina and hefted her. She hugged back, hating it when he pulled away.

"Praise God," Mathias said, falling to his knees and kissing a rock.

Pa nodded but focused his attention upward through a gap in the tree-tops, relishing the wind in the pines. The clouds had cleared a little, exposing cerulean blue skies, gifting them with a glimpse of heaven and embracing them in the harmonies of high nature. "Amen, Father."

Strobridge still favored his right leg, but didn't appear to be shot or bit or bleeding. He looked half the man they'd met in the street two days ago. His fine jacket was torn, his shirt caked with dirt and dried blood. His kerchief hung loose around his neck.

"I guess this is where we part ways, Mister Strobridge," Mathias said to the railroad boss.

"No need to part ways, Thomas. Might be a good idea to have some company on the road back."

"We'll be fine," Manning said.

"Red and me can scare up just about anything in these forests and mountains," Buck added. "We should have something on the spit by nightfall. Provided the deaduns remain in relative disarray for the next day or so, we can make it back to Coburn or Truckee or whatever the fuck they're calling it these days before too long."

Strobridge scratched at his beard. "I'll pay every one of you for protection."

Father Mathias frowned, but it was Nina who spoke first. "None of us want your filthy fucking money."

"Nina," Pa admonished.

Strobridge went silent a moment, then his eyes grew fierce again. "Suit yourselves then. Me and my boys will race you to the top and leave you to rot with those walking corpses. Let's go."

George and Mason looked at one another, but didn't move, each waiting for the other to take the initial step, Nina reckoned.

Manning spoke up, "You think these Daggett *boys* are gonna help you at the first sign of wolves or a bear?"

George Daggett scratched at the scruff on his face. "Mase, you seen any bears out here?"

Mason gazed stonily at Manning. "Not yet."

"Black bears aplenty in these mountains, you idiots," said Pa.

Strobridge's brow sprouted sweat, his eyes passing between vicious and worried, finally coming to a decision on which tact to take. "Look, we were wrong. We admit it. But if you had that crazy Chinese bastard after you, you'd have wanted to get out, too. He knows I have the Taiping Jing, so not like I had much choice. Maybe we acted out of sorts—"

"That's a fucking understatement," Buck said.

"We could have used you to fight Liao," Manning said. "Because he *didn't* go after you, he came after us. Had we stuck together, maybe we'd have had a chance to keep Miss Buell and the marshal from getting killed."

Father Mathias cut in. "Tell you what. Hand over the Taiping Jing, and we'll help you get to your train."

"What's the alternative?"

Mathias shared a long look with Manning before shrugging. "No alternative."

"Jesus H. Christ! Fine. You can have the goddamn thing. Just get me the fuck to my train."

"Which direction?" Manning said.

Strobridge looked up into the sky and all around, eyes dropping to follow Maples Creek where it twisted out of view amongst the rocky outcrops and towering conifers. "We follow the creek east and then south…"

Pa's brow furrowed as he remembered. "I know some trails down to Coburn that should be easy enough to traverse."

"Good. Like I said, east and then south until we hit the tracks. Then follow them west back down into Truckee where our glorious train awaits." Strobridge peered south, taking in the stark, snow-blanketed peaks jutting up like teeth on a serrated blade. "I hope y'all are ready for a climb."

Nina noticed Woodie sitting alone on a rock down by the creek. His shoulders jerked as he sobbed, his hand slowly moving from the water to his face.

In a way, Nina could see how the guy had been recruited by Strobridge, lied to, taken advantage of, and who knew what else? Her own people had been hard on him, too, especially Manning, worse than Strobridge in some ways.

She went over, squatting next to him on a rock. "Hey, you okay?"

Woodie raised his head. Nina gasped. Both eyes were nearly swollen shut, both lips puffed out and creased with cuts. His cheeks were bruised and split, and a piece of flesh hung from his brow where Manning's knuckle must have connected good. Judging from the blood coming out of his mouth, he was missing several teeth, too.

"Duh it loo' li' mm uh-hay?" He splashed a handful of water on his face, let a line of bloody drool hang from his lips.

"Is there anything I can do? Red Thunder has—"

"Lee me tha fuhg uh-wone. Din ath you people fo'nuthin. Din ath fo'elp, din ath tuh be pard uh thith. Juth lee me uh-wone." He glared at Strobridge. "Tha goeth fo' him, too."

Nina nodded and raised her hands. "Look, it's been hard these past few days. On all of us. I just want to apologize. Probably doesn't mean shit to you. I get it. But I'm sorry. I mean…you didn't deserve this." She gestured to his face.

Woodie nodded, sputtering more bloody water, but the uneasy look in his eyes told her he didn't buy a damn word of it.

Nina held his shoulder for a moment, gave it a reassuring squeeze, stood and walked away.

The click of a cocking revolver froze her. A gunshot cracked the sky, jerking her shoulders together in fright. Birds took flight from the trees as something heavy fell over behind her.

She turned to see Woodie lying dead, her own Colt Navy limp in his hand. Nina grasped at her empty holster as the waters of Maples Creek ran over Woodie's boots. The top of his head was a grizzly mess of twisted skull and bloody hair.

"Shit."

EPILOGUE

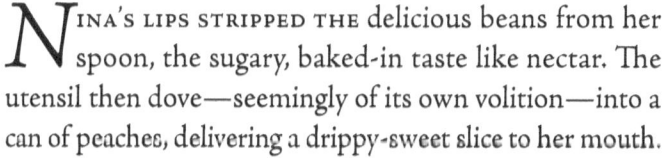

Nina's lips stripped the delicious beans from her spoon, the sugary, baked-in taste like nectar. The utensil then dove—seemingly of its own volition—into a can of peaches, delivering a drippy-sweet slice to her mouth.

They dined. That was the best way to put it. A grand oak table smack in the middle of the dining car, built for Strobridge by some fellow named Crocker, now perfectly suitable for an orphan, a whore, a half-breed Injun, and a wounded old man.

Mathias was there, too, sitting on the leather window couch reading from a Bible he'd found in one of the desk drawers, sipping on a 'particularly spectacular and not unreliable' brand of whiskey from a snifter. No matter what, the priest was the picture of calm. Even now he lounged

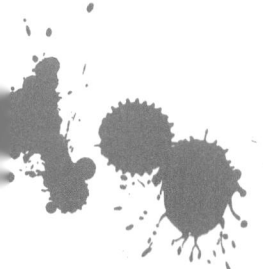

in his black robes, one leg thrown over his knee, his head tossed back as he read through wire-framed spectacles perched on his nose. In his lap rested this cryptic Taiping Jing; what amounted to an ornamental, golden key, as far as Nina could tell.

How he hadn't gorged on vittles by now was beyond her.

She caught Jasmine's eye across the table, warmed by the woman's beaming smile. After a few mouthfuls, Jasmine sat by the window and sung, her voice strong and resonant, hopeful. Yet her despondent words came from some dark distant place Nina suspected was far south. Rachel sat next to her, listening. The girl had refused food, despite the fact she had to be starving. Pa worked on a can of carrots, his face all contented bliss, his ankle wrapped and forgotten for the moment.

Empty cans had been piled in the middle, ten or twelve of them, victims all.

They relaxed to the slow chug of the steam engine, the *chu-chu, chu-chu* as the cranks churned, the iron beast coming alive all around them. But this was *their* beast, and at the moment, they were safe and happy.

Occasionally, a deadun thumped against the carriage, but this car was well-armored, Strobridge's idea to thwart Indians and raiders as he traveled back and forth down the line between San Francisco and some place called Reno, the latter being their current destination.

Nina went to where the whiskey crates were stacked and pulled out a bottle; brand spanking new. The entire right side of the car had cupboards full of food and other pleasantries, jugs full of various liquors, and even a lavatory to wash in.

Nina opened the cabin door and watched the ground pass slowly beneath her. She stepped across the threshold to the tender car, climbing the ladder to the top and walking its full, rumbling length before dropping down the other side and into the cab of Engine 141, the *Magpie*—leastways that's what it said on the side of the steel beast.

Buck and Strobridge went over a series of levers and controls while Manning and Mason threw shovels of coal into the belly of the beast. Strobridge had turned out to be more than just a piece of shit railroad boss. He knew the train like the back of his hand. Sleeves rolled up, he'd oiled her intricate parts up and down her sides, checking lines and making sure she was ready to run.

James looked like a mountain god with his shirt off, covered in sweat and coal dust. Mason wasn't half bad himself, except he was a Daggett. Between turns, James gave her that lopsided smile of his. For a second, Nina saw a childish side of him, or rather, what he might have been like as a child. Good-natured, probably. Hair lighter blond then, thin and tall early on but broadening out later. He'd probably loved his mama. She'd have to ask him later.

Nina gave him a wave, set the bottle of whiskey inside the door, and went back to car three. By this time, Jasmine and Rachel had joined Father Mathias on the leather couch as the priest read aloud from his book. Pa watched and listened from the table. He smiled at her and nodded. He looked beat.

Nina returned her pa's smile, then plucked out two more bottles and headed for the last car, an armored behemoth meant to dismantle anyone who had the balls to hijack them. George Daggett stood up in the turret, messing with the small cannon perched there. When he heard Nina come in, he gave her a curt nod, a large bruise had formed on his cheekbone where Manning had clocked him with the Spencer. She held up the bottle of whiskey, and a smile lit his face.

"Truce?"

He reached down for the bottle. "Why not?"

Red Thunder was sorting through the stockpile of munitions Strobridge had outfitted prior to all hell breaking loose. He seemed glad to see her, which was a step better than the grunt of admonishment he normally produced.

"You see here?" Red Thunder ran his hand along the side of the ironclad car, putting his hands into slits. "Loop holes to shoot from. And we have guns, and more ammunition than we can use. We are well prepared."

Nina sat down on a box of supplies while he worked. *U.S. ARMY* was stenciled on many of the containers and she suppressed her deep-seated emotions upon seeing those words.

"Can I share something with you, brother?"

"Yes."

"I felt it. The spirit of my people. Well, moments here and there." She told him about the dream she had, her talk with the boha gande and what he'd said about her mother watching over her. She related the times she'd heard the drums, and how they'd helped her be strong.

"That is good, Ninataku. But..." The Indian hesitated, putting his hand on her shoulder as if he could transfer understanding through touch alone.

"What?"

"You are still resisting, afraid of the power. You are

fearful of failing."

Nina shook her head, confused and little annoyed. "What's that mean? We were just trying to survive, me and Pa. All of us."

"Surviving is not enough, Ninataku. Not now. Let the spirits of your people in, and you will see. Perhaps you have yet to bond with your weyekin. I don't know."

"Tell me how to find it."

"You will not find it. It will find you. Young warriors go into the forest or mountains to find theirs, searching sometimes for days, some of them never returning. You only need to have an open heart when the time comes."

Nina's spirit took flight. "You think I can be a warrior?" Not only was Red Thunder's insinuation flattering, but it was unheard of for a woman to be given such status in the tribe.

"You are already a warrior, Ninataku." Then he chuckled, as if amused at some inside joke. "A warrior with no spirit guide."

She frowned and left the car, sliding the heavy compartment door open to stand on the observation deck of the train. The station receded into the distance as Coburn/Truckee faded behind a copse of trees just north of the tracks. It was a dead town now, still smoldering in sooty streaks, which drifted into the sky. She hoped it *stayed* buried.

Nina opened the other bottle of whiskey, lifted it, and took a long chug. It burned her throat on the way down, but she welcomed the cleansing heat. She held up the bottle and took another drink, this one for Woodie.

While she didn't regret the things she'd done over the

past few days to survive, she knew the deaths of Grover and Clara Buell, Marshal Oden, and Woodie Woodruff would stick with her for a bit. All had been good people at heart...well, the Buells and the marshal, at least. She was less certain of Woodie, yet she chose to believe he was good on the inside, just tormented. His passing was made even darker by its cause. But she couldn't blame Manning. Couldn't blame anyone. Men were just bad, or good, in varying degrees, depending on one's point of view.

Nina would have to be very careful in the coming days, but she felt stronger now than she'd ever felt.

The compartment door slid open, and James Manning came to stand next to her. She passed him the bottle. Together they watched the world roll by, the train cutting through a swath of trees, and then up along a clear ridge whose sides plunged straight down fifty feet. The base was sparsely populated by deaduns.

One decomposing fellow raised his arms and stumbled toward them, trying to climb the grade to reach the train. Nina waved back. Manning's confused expression made her snort.

"What?" he said.

"Sorry, just trying to lighten up after all the hell we been through."

Manning's grin shone through his handsome coal-covered face. "Nothing wrong with that." He leaned over the rail and spat.

As they gained speed, the trails of coal smoke and steam exhaust billowed out behind them, making fat plumes in the sky.

"We agreed not to go too fast. Never know what kinds

of surprises Liao has ahead. Would hate to hit a piece of track with no rails. Wouldn't be hard to sabotage us."

"Let's hope not." Nina leaned on the rail, too, so that their elbows touched. If Manning noticed, he didn't let on.

"Can you believe this train? Even got a shitter."

"It's incredible. My first time on one."

"I've been on them plenty, but never part of a rail team. There's a lot to learn. We'd have never made it out without Strobridge, much as I hate to admit. He seems to know this train like he's lived in one his whole life. Guess I should say thanks for not shooting him."

"You're welcome." After a pause, she added, "Wonder what's waiting for us in Reno?"

Manning gave her more than a quick glance, his eyes lingering, burning against her skin. Nina started to meet his gaze, but he'd already looked away.

"Don't know. Don't care. As long as I can get in a good long sleep between here and there. Strobridge says first thing we get there he'll telegraph his people and we should do the same, warn whoever we can, then go as far east as possible."

"Sounds like a plan." Nina grinned, unable to stop herself from wrapping her hand under Manning's arm and putting her cheek against his shoulder. Nervous as an apple thief, her pulse raced and her gut somersaulted. *What was he thinking?*

It didn't take long for her to find out. He stood up. "I've got something I want to ask you."

Nina faced him, taking in his dirty face, the scabs and the scruff, and the eager look in his eyes. Their bodies thrummed with energy as their arms intertwined. "Yes?"

James leaned into her, arms wrapping her up and pulling her tight against him. His lips descended, and she rose to meet him as the train rolled on, and on, and on.

AUTHORS' NOTES

IN LATE APRIL 2013, I sent a chat message to Demon Squad author Tim Marquitz saying we should collaborate on something. We had become friends through a group I started up in 2010 called The Writers of the Storm, and we were arsing about, just chatting online. I was joking, of course, and expected the answer to be, "Yeah, right," since Tim's actually busier than I am. So imagine my grin when he replied, "We absolutely should." And then came his next chat message: "What do you want to do?"

Going back a couple months prior, to mid-February, a fella named Michael Wheeler had written to me online, saying, "hey, you should write a zombie western! There's really only one good one out there ("Exit Humanity") but nothing really great." It was a cool idea, this "Night of the

Living Dead" meets "The Battle of the Alamo" thing, but that was pretty much it. I was in the midst of launching Nine Worlds Media, so I figured I'd shelf that and get to it someday, but the idea stuck in my craw and kind of got my wheels turning. It just would not let me be.

So when Tim asked, "What do you want to do?" I had my answer ready and waiting.

A Western. Featuring *zombies*.

Over the next hour we discussed more details, coming up with the main character, who I thought should be a Native American half-breed with a hard as nails exterior, savvy, guarded, but also damaged and vulnerable. I also threw out that I'd like a graycoat or two, a gunslinger, and a missionary priest. Those were things I already had in mind when the aforementioned wheels were turning. So this gave us an idea of the timeframe, something fresh on the heels of the American Civil War.

At some point, Tim asked me if I thought Kenny Soward would be interested in being part of it. Kenny has been my friend for a long time, but I knew he had his nose to the keyboard writing his fantasy series, GnomeSaga, so I figured he'd be too busy—though I also knew he was a sucker for zombies. I lobbed the idea at him, and he mentioned it was peculiar timing because he'd been thinking a lot about writing a zombie series anyway, and here one was just dropped into his lap.

The three of us brainstormed a bit more and decided that it had to have trains in it, especially since both Kenny and I are fans of the AMC series "Hell on Wheels."

Anyone acquainted with Tim knows he's really

passionate about writing, so it should not have surprised me that next morning when I had a full outline of the *Untitled Zombie Western* in my inbox. He had incorporated everything we had discussed and then-some. I read it with a stupid grin, absolutely loved it, shared it with Kenny, and like that, we were full steam ahead.

The collaborative process has worked out great. We give and take energy from one another, share ideas, use social media to stay connected constantly, and we're all very impressed with one another's work, patting one another on the back when need be, and relentlessly giving one another shit to keep things light; plus none of us have egos about our work (ask any one of us and we'll tell you we suck!) so we've all been open-minded about the give and take—pertaining to revisions and amended details—and the various responsibilities we've doled out to one another. The process constantly fed the hopper, firing up the imagination train and chugging right along.

Those Poor, Poor Bastards (TPPB), would not be what it is without Kenny. Tim and I both readily admit that, and it was a genius move on our parts to turn our ambitious two-way into a rapturous three-way. The guy is a machine and he embraced the role of 'wordmonkey' with full-on temerity, cranking daily, always dedicated to making his word count quota, which is how the project came together so quickly.

Another advantage is that I poured myself into the research and shared my findings with the guys. I picked the Sierra Nevadas during the expansion of the Transcontinental Railroad as our setting, specifically a trade town called Coburn Station (modern day Truckee, CA) as our starting point.

I frequented websites like the California State Railroad Museum (csrmf.org), Central Pacific Railroad Photographic History Museum (cprr.org), The First Transcontinental Railroad (tcrr.com), and PBS.org. I researched the principal men involved in the building of the railroads, as well as the surrounding areas geologically and socio-politically. This was a hell of a tumultuous time, and although of course this is a fictionalization, I felt I'd be doing a disservice if I didn't ensure our details were accurate as they could be.

Putting the historical details aside, the characters just really came to life as things unfolded. There's nothing like an extreme survival situation to bring out extreme personalities. If you don't root for our heroic protagonist Nina Weaver and her pa, Lincoln; if you don't feel for those poor Buells; if you're not put off yet randomly amused by the Daggetts; if you don't despise J.H. Strobridge; if you're not a little bit fascinated by the depth of James Manning, the mystery of Father Mathias, the stoicism of Red Thunder, the resilience of Jasmine and Rachel Buell, the valor of Marshal Oden, the gruffness of Buck Patterson, and the misfortune of Les Woodruff, then I guess you deserve your money back.

Anyhow, so that's where we're at, and I imagine you're asking, "What's next?" If so, good news. We have a fully-imagined Weird Western supernatural horror adventure crowded with a mash-'em-up of pseudo-Lovecraftian/Clive Barkerian monsters and mutants.

So, yes, more Dead West. Tim, Kenny, and I have conceptualized a six-part saga, with each installment coming in at more or less the same size as TPPB. That's six novels, available as eBooks and in print. How does that strike you? Oh, good! Glad to hear you're on board… because the three of us love having you. Thanks for visiting our imaginations. We're indebted to ya, and we'll keep aiming to please.

J.M. Martin
July 9, 2013
Crestview Hills, KY

D EAD WEST WAS ONE of those projects I lucked into. Never really pictured myself getting neck-deep into a western, let alone a zombie western, but when Joe approached me, wanting to do something together, it was an opportunity I couldn't pass up. It evolved from there. His excitement was infectious.

Joe's one of those overlooked authors (editor/artist) whose talents have yet to be recognized by the world at large, which is a shame. His attention to detail and manic commitment to a project is humbling, and the quality of his efforts shine through.

It was one of these efforts that drew my eye: his editing and cover design on Kenny Soward's Rough Magic. Combined with Kenny's amazing writing and characterization, Rough Magic stood out in a way very few self-published releases do. I was enthralled by the book. And as it turns out, Joe and Kenny are friends, and

I knew immediately I wanted to include Kenny in the mix. Fortunately, it only took a tiny bit of wheedling to get him involved. As soon as he was onboard, "Dead West" exploded.

Those Poor, Poor Bastards is the end result of our devious union, and I'm insanely proud of it. I learned a lot from Joe and Kenny, both more than earning my respect and awe. The first foray into "Dead West" was a terrific experience, which I hope translates through the page to you, the reader.

Welcome to the ride.

Tim Marquitz
July 11, 2013
El Paso, TX

WHEN JOE AND TIM approached me about Dead West series, I initially thought it might be a bit too much for me at the time. I was halfway done with book two of the GnomeSaga, The Tinkermage, and I'd intended to really bear down on it. Also, I've been around the block a few times, and I usually know when to say no. But this project had me intrigued. I'd been working with Joe professionally for more than a year—although we're high school classmates—and didn't know Tim very well except he had quite a few books out (one of which I'd read). I knew Tim was very talented, and I appreciated the support he gave me while I published Rough Magic. All these factors had me leaning toward a yes.

Then it struck me that a change from fantasy to a rough-

and-tumble Wild West horror piece might just be the thing I needed to shake things up between my fantasy novels. Plus, I love a challenge. So, I gave it a thumbs up.

I found the daily adventure of collaborating quite fun: the constant cutting up, the professionalism, and the drive to make this series the best we could. I genuinely looked up to Tim and Joe and learned a great deal from both of them throughout this entire process. We had so much fun working on the project that we're chomping at the bit to get started on book two.

Strap yourselves in. It's going to be a wild ride!

Kenny Soward
July 11, 2013
Independence, KY

ABOUT THE AUTHORS

*R*AISED ON A DIET of Heavy Metal and bad intentions, Tim Marquitz writes a mix of the dark perverse, the horrific, and the tragic, tinged with sarcasm and biting humor. A former grave digger, bouncer, and dedicated metalhead, he is a huge fan of Mixed Martial Arts, and fighting in general. His urban fantasy series called Demon Squad is a fan favorite and he is also the Editor-In-Chief of Ragnarok Publications. He lives in El Paso, Texas, with his beautiful wife and daughter.

His website is www.tmarquitz.com.

J.M. MARTIN HAS BEEN a teacher, an occupational therapist, a managing editor, and a graphic designer. He wrote comic books for Caliber Comics and role-playing games for Privateer Press, as well as several short stories for Fantasist Enterprises, Rogue Blades Entertainment, Pill Hill Press, and Angelic Knight Press. He recently co-founded Ragnarok Publications with Tim Marquitz and is the company's Creative Director.

J.M. (Joe) lives in Crestview Hills, Kentucky, with his fiery-haired, black belt wife and three spirited wee folk he refers to affectionately as *homunculi*.

Find him on Facebook and Twitter (@martinjm70).

KENNY SOWARD GREW UP in Crescent Park, Kentucky, a small suburb just south of Cincinnati, Ohio, listening to AC/DC, Quiet Riot, and Iron Maiden. In those quiet 1970's streets, he jumped bikes, played Nerf football, and acquired many a childhood scar. At the age of sixteen, he learned to play drums and bashed skins for many groups over the next twenty years.

By day, Kenny works as a Unix professional, and at night he writes and sips bourbon. His fantasy series GnomeSaga is published by Ragnarok Publications. He lives in Independence, Kentucky, with two cats and a gal who thinks she's a cat.

Visit him online and watch his awesomely entertaining videos at www.kennysoward.com.

THANK YOU

For purchasing this book!
Visit our website to see more titles in:
Speculative Fiction
Dark Fantasy
Urban Fantasy
Supernatural Horror
Short Story Collections
All penned by some of the bestselling authors and
talented up-and-comers writing high-quality genre
fiction today.

Please post reviews at online stores and review sites.
Your opinion matters to us!

www.ragnarokpub.com

www.ingramcontent.com/pod-product-compliance
Lightning Source LLC
Chambersburg PA
CBHW032123170626
46808CB00006B/2079